STROKE THE FLAME

HER ELEMENTAL DRAGONS BOOK ONE

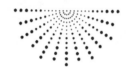

ELIZABETH BRIGGS

For all the girls who wanted to save the world too

1

KIRA

I crept through the forest in search of my prey, my hand tight on my bow. Heavy rain left a sheen of water on my face even with my hood covering me, and I wiped it off on my already-soaked sleeve. The storm was getting stronger. If I didn't find a deer or something else soon, I'd have to give up and return empty-handed. Roark wouldn't like that.

I made my way toward one of my traps up ahead, stepping carefully through the high brush and keeping my eyes peeled for any game. With the weather as it was, I doubted I would have any luck. All the animals in the forest had no doubt retreated once this sudden storm had come upon us. The only thing left out here would be elementals and shades —and I had no desire to confront either of those.

When I'd set out a few hours ago, the sky had been clear and bright. Only in the last hour had the storm clouds gathered overhead as if out of nowhere, or perhaps summoned by the Gods themselves. I shivered, and not just from the cold that sank into my bones through my soaked clothes.

I bent down to check the trap I'd left this morning and breathed a sigh of relief. A large rabbit had been caught inside. Tonight I'd be fed. Tonight Tash would be safe.

I tossed the rabbit into a sack and loaded it onto my shoulder. When I turned around, I wasn't alone. I dropped the sack and aimed my bow, my heart in my throat.

An old woman stood before me, her body hunched over with age, her skin pale and wrinkled. She wore a frayed traveling cloak and frizzy white hair escaped her low hood. I might have heard her as she approached, but the storm drowned out all sound except for the pounding of rain in the trees.

"Can I help you?" I called out to her, as I lowered my bow and retrieved my fallen sack.

"Perhaps." She stared at me and frowned, then looked around as if confused.

"You must be lost. I can show you to Stoneham, the nearest town."

"That's kind of you."

I offered her my arm and she took it, leaning upon me. Her grip was strong, even though she seemed so frail I worried a strong gust might turn her bones to dust. I wondered how she had found herself in the middle of the forest in the first place. She shouldn't be traveling alone, especially not in this weather.

"What's your name?" she asked.

"Kira."

As we carefully stepped through the forest she gazed up at the dark sky, letting the rain wash over her face. "There's a storm coming."

I patted her wrinkled hand where it rested on my arm. "I think it's already here. But if we hurry, we can get out of it. The inn is just ahead."

"There's no escaping this storm." She turned toward me and her eyes were like steel. "Not for you."

Her words sent another shiver down my spine. "I'm not sure what you mean."

She held my gaze another few seconds, then waved her hand. "Just the ramblings of an old woman. Nothing more."

I frowned, but continued walking through the wet brush. "We're nearly there now."

"Yes, indeed we are," she said.

A rustling sound up ahead caught my attention. I dropped her arm and drew my bow. "Stay back. I'll make sure the way is clear."

I took a step forward as I peered through the brush in front of us, watching for the slightest twitch of a leaf or the dash of fur. But there was nothing other than the relentless rain.

When I turned back, the woman was gone.

"Hello?" I called out, spinning around and scanning the area for her. The storm made it hard to see anything, but there was no trace of her anywhere. She'd just...vanished.

I went back the way we'd walked, calling out for the woman, but I couldn't find her anywhere. There was no sign she'd ever been in the forest at all.

After many long minutes, with the rain pounding down on me and the wind whipping at my cloak, I reluctantly gave up my search. I told myself she must have gone ahead to the village without me, but something about that didn't feel right. It was the only explanation though, unless she was a shade. But if that were true I wouldn't still be breathing, according to the stories I'd heard anyway. I'd never actually seen a shade before, but it was said they were ghostly figures that could turn invisible, pass through walls, and suck the life right out of you. As strange as the woman was, she seemed perfectly human at least. Still, probably best for me to hurry back.

I headed toward the inn, more by instinct than sight at this point. As I left the forest, my shoes sank into the mud and the relentless wind tore the hood off my head. I tried to tug it back on, but there was no use. My hair was already soaked through and I was chilled to the bone.

Lightning flashed overhead, followed immediately by the deep rumble of thunder. I ran for the inn as fast as I could, but the wind was so strong it seemed to push me back, as if it was fighting my every step. I slipped in the mud and fell to my knees, bracing myself with my hands. The impact jolted through my bones, and for a moment I could only remain there, dazed and covered in mud from head to toe.

As I tried to stand, a bright crack lit up the sky, blinding me. Searing hot pain struck my head and I screamed as a bolt of lightning coursed through me. Electricity spread within my entire body, setting every nerve on fire and burning me from the inside out. It raced through my blood, and I thought my heart would burst from the power warring for control within me. Time stopped, and pain became the only thing I knew.

And then it was gone.

Deep, cavernous thunder sounded all around me as my sight returned. My entire body shook and trembled uncontrollably. Mud covered me completely, rain pelted my face, wind lashed at my hair, and sparks danced in my blood. As if the elemental Gods themselves had thought to strike me down, then decided to let me live after all.

I scrambled back to my feet, nearly slipping again in the slick mud. When I was steady, I grabbed the bag with the rabbit from where I'd dropped it, before stumbling to the back door of the inn. I opened the door with some effort, the wind battling me still, and then stepped inside the familiar warm kitchen that smelled of stew and baked bread. Once the door was shut, I fell back against it, breathing heavily.

I'd been struck by lightning. Yet somehow I still lived.

I quickly checked my body, searching for signs of injury, but I seemed to be physically fine, although my cloak was charred and I was in great need of a bath. The only thing that afflicted me was shock.

None of it made sense. Lightning usually hit the tallest thing around, and I was nowhere near that. I'd been surrounded by much better targets. The inn. The stables. The trees. Why had it hit me?

And how had I made it through without a scratch?

2

KIRA

"Kira?" a friendly voice called out. My best friend, Tash, who worked as a waitress in her father's inn and tavern. Like most of the people in the Earth Realm, she had dark skin and thick black hair, which she often wore in a braid, and with her cheerful smile she made even the drabbest apron look good. She rushed over to me and gasped. "You poor thing. You're completely soaked and look like you went mud wrestling with the pigs. Come in out of the cold and we'll get you something to warm you up."

"I'm all right," I said, but it wasn't very convincing. I'm pretty sure my teeth chattered. "Just need to change my clothes."

Tash bit her lip, but nodded. "Did you get anything?"

"Yeah." I handed her the bag with the rabbit. It wasn't much, but it would have to do. Between the elemental attacks on nearby farms and the Black Dragon's taxes, food was scarce these days. Something Roark reminded us of often.

Her face softened with relief. "Thank the Gods."

I snorted. "The Gods have abandoned us. Thank me for setting up the traps in advance."

She chuckled. "Go clean yourself up, you're tracking mud all over the kitchen. Mother's going to have a fit."

I stepped out of the kitchen and into the small room behind it, where I currently lived. Roark, Tash's father, owned this inn and allowed me to stay here as long as I caught him some game and fetched some herbs and spices from the forest. If I brought something back, I got to eat that night. If not, I didn't. If I missed two days in a row, he'd beat Tash in punishment. Oh, originally he'd tried to beat me, but I hadn't cared. I'd suffered much worse before. He soon realized it hurt me more to beat his own daughter, my one true friend.

I'd never missed two days in a row again.

I quickly stripped off my soiled cloak, along with the rest of my hunting leathers, then changed into a simple blue dress with frayed edges. I exchanged my muddy boots for my one pair of dull slippers. Nothing could be done for my wet, crusty hair, which was more brown than red at the moment, but I tried smoothing it down anyway and wiped away the dried dirt.

Once again, I checked myself for any signs of injury, but there seemed to be no lasting damage from my brush with death. Even so, I sank onto the narrow bed and rubbed my eyes with trembling hands, willing the sense of dread to leave me. Between the old woman's words and the lightning strike, my twentieth birthday was definitely not going as I'd hoped.

After pulling myself together, I returned to the kitchen. Tash herded me into the tavern, to the lone empty table in the corner. "Sit here," she said. "I'll fetch you something to eat."

"Thanks." I gave her arm a quick squeeze before she slipped away.

The inn was packed with soldiers and travelers trying to avoid the storm, and the air had a humid, musky scent. I quickly scanned the room, but the old lady wasn't in sight. Perhaps she'd already gone to her room to rest. I ducked my eyes when one of the Black Dragon's soldiers on duty gave me a stern look. They were always watching from behind their winged helmets and scaled black armor, ready to enforce her rule. The green markings on their shoulders signaled they were in the Earth Realm division of the Onyx Army, under the command of the Jade Dragon.

At the bar, a couple travelers were speaking in hushed tones, but the word "elemental" drifted over to me and caught my attention. I leaned forward, straining to hear the rest.

"Miners dug too deep and angered those big rock elementals," a man wearing a dark green cloak said. "They smashed up the town pretty good before they were finally driven off."

"Aren't the Dragons supposed to deal with those?" another man muttered into his tankard.

A woman with a red scarf around her neck snorted quietly. "They're too busy collecting taxes and trying to stomp out the Resistance."

"I saw the Crimson Dragon the other day in the next village over," another man said, making my back stiffen. "Flying overhead like he was looking for something. Or someone."

The woman glanced warily at the nearby soldier before whispering, "I heard the Golden one was in Pebbleton a week ago."

"We never get Dragons this far from Soulspire. Why now?" the first man asked.

The second man downed his drink with a sour look. "The Black Dragon is demanding more tribute than ever before. Her Dragons are there to make sure we obey. Or else."

Cold fear gripped my throat. If the Dragons were nearby, that meant it was time for me to leave Stoneham. And soon.

I'd seen two Dragons in my life and never wanted to see one again. The screams and smell of burning flesh still haunted my dreams, but Stoneham had been safe so far. I'd been here since I was seventeen, living in the back of the inn that Tash's family owned while keeping my head down and staying out of trouble. This town was at the very edge of the Earth Realm, far enough away from Soulspire that the Black Dragon and her mates never flew out this far.

Until now.

Tash set down a steaming bowl of rabbit stew and a

tankard of mead, along with a small cake she'd decorated with white frosting. "Here you are!"

"What's this?" I asked, arching an eyebrow at the cake.

"It's for your birthday, of course. You didn't really expect me to forget, did you?" She flashed me a warm smile.

"Thank you, Tash." I hadn't wanted her to make a big deal about my birthday, but I appreciated that she remembered it. She was the closest thing I had to family, after all.

She bent down and gave me a quick hug. "Happy birthday."

I hugged her back. "Hey, did you see an older woman come through here with white hair? I stumbled upon her in the forest, but then I lost her."

"No, but I've been in the kitchen all night. Father probably took her up to a room already."

"I hope so. I don't like the idea of her being out there alone." Something about the encounter tugged at my gut with a sense of wrongness, but I couldn't put my finger on it.

Tash squeezed my shoulder. "If you didn't see her out there, then she must be safe inside somewhere. Maybe she's staying with family in town."

"I'm sure you're right," I said, trying to banish my unease as I took a bite of my cake. "Mm. This is delicious."

"Of course it is." She winked, but then was called away to another table. I watched her go and sadness clenched my heart tight. I didn't want to leave Stoneham. Tash was my best friend, and more than that, she needed me. If I was gone, who would protect her from her father?

Perhaps she would come with me if I left. But no, she

would never leave her mother behind. Maybe it was only a coincidence the Dragons had been spotted nearby. Maybe they would never come to Stoneham.

Maybe I didn't have to run. At least, not yet.

A commotion and a shout at the bar drew my attention. Two of the soldiers hauled the man in the green cloak off his stool and shoved him to the ground, while the woman cried out, "We were just talking! We didn't mean anything by it!"

I watched with dread, my stomach twisting at the knowledge of what would happen next. I'd seen it before, and no matter how much I wanted to help those people or stop the soldiers, there was nothing I could do. I knew how to defend myself a little, but not against two armored soldiers with swords as long as my arm. The only reason I'd made it this long was by keeping my head down and staying out of trouble. But that didn't stop me from wishing there was something I could do to stop this.

One of the soldiers grabbed the woman's wrist and dragged her off the stool too. "Sounds to me like you're part of the Resistance. Don't you agree, Ment?"

The other soldier nodded, while a cruel smile touched his lips. "That it does. And we all know how we deal with Resistance scum."

The cloaked man shook his head vehemently. "We're not Resistance! We're loyal to the Black Dragon, I swear it!"

"Tell that to the Spirit Goddess when you see her," Ment said, as he hauled the man to his feet.

Roark glared at them from behind the bar and rubbed his hands on a towel, but said nothing. The soldiers gave him a nod as they led the two struggling people out of the inn. The door shut, and the entire room froze as a howling scream tore through the sound of the rain, before it was cut short. With grim faces, the other people in the tavern returned to their meals and their conversation, including the other man who'd been talking with the doomed travelers. Maybe we were all cowards, but it was the only way to survive.

I dropped my head as shame and despair battled inside me, along with the keen realization that there was no point in running. No matter where I went, there was no escaping the Dragons or their soldiers.

3

KIRA

I had the first dream that night.

A roguishly handsome man with hair the color of autumn leaves drew a large sword, then lunged at an opponent. Both of them wore the black-scaled armor of the Onyx Army with the red shoulder markings of the Fire Realm division. A small crowd had gathered around them as they sparred, but the auburn-haired man was the only one I could see clearly. Even though I hated the Black Dragon's soldiers, I found I couldn't tear my eyes away from him, nor banish the unexpected desire he stirred inside me. As I watched, he dodged, parried, and swiftly disarmed his opponent, winning the training match without breaking a sweat. He bowed to his opponent, and when he rose up, I caught a flash of flame in his brown eyes.

When I woke my skin was so hot I had to throw the

blanket off me. I was certain I'd never seen him before in my life—I would have remembered a man that attractive. I wasn't sure what the fire in his eyes meant either. The only man who could control flame was Sark, the Crimson Dragon, and that wasn't him. I'd never forget *that* monster's face.

I brushed it off as merely a strange dream, a result of my loneliness and nothing more, and forced myself to go back to sleep. But the next night, I had another dream. This one featured a different man who stood in a library wearing some of the finest clothes I'd ever seen. Clearly a nobleman of some sort, with golden hair, fair skin, and a finely sculpted face I wouldn't mind staring at for hours. He was extremely tall, but as he reached for a book on a very high shelf, his fingers barely touched it. A burst of wind suddenly swirled around him, and the book dropped into his hand.

Impossible. I'd never seen the Golden Dragon before, but somehow I knew this wasn't him. But if not, how could this man control the element of air? Only the Dragons, the representatives of the elemental Gods, were blessed with such power. Including the Black Dragon, of course—their wife and our supreme ruler.

It was nonsense, I told myself. Simply my dream brain coming up with strange images because I'd been worried about the Dragons coming for me. That was all.

But the dreams continued.

One night I encountered a ruggedly handsome green-eyed man with dark skin, a trim beard, and a broad chest. With muscular arms he hammered a sword, but when he raised it up I swore the metal bent by nothing more than the power of his mind. I had the strongest urge to run to him and bury my face in his strong chest, knowing he would protect me with his every breath.

In the next dream, I saw a black-haired man who exuded danger slip through the forest like a wraith. Rain battered against the leaves, yet somehow left him untouched. He pulled down his hood, and I caught a flash of sharp, deadly beauty. Upon awakening, my entire body was doused in cold sweat. Like the others, he filled me with a strange sense of desire and longing I couldn't understand or explain.

Every night I was visited by one of my strange elemental dream men, although they never seemed to know I was there spying on them. Soon they all began to travel, though I couldn't tell where they were headed or why. All I got were brief glimpses into their lives without any real context. Or whatever lives my mind was inventing for them, anyway— none of them were real, of course. Even if I began to secretly wish they were.

The traveling dreams were clearly a sign I should be on my way as well, yet I hesitated. A month passed. I told myself I needed more time. Time to gather my coins. Time to learn more about the Dragons' intentions. Time to make sure Tash would be okay.

But I was only delaying the inevitable.

~

"Heard there's a Fire Realm soldier in the tavern," the fletcher said, as I handed him my coins in exchange for more arrows.

My fingers clenched around my bow. "A Fire Realm soldier? Here?"

"That's what Brant said when he dropped off the wood. Seems like the soldier's looking for someone. Searching for Resistance members maybe?" He shrugged.

I stiffened. "None of us have anything to do with them. Everyone knows we all serve the Black Dragon loyally."

"I'm sure he's just passing through." He frowned and glanced at the door warily, where two Earth Realm soldiers could be seen patrolling the town. "Still, I'll be glad when he's on his way."

"Me too."

It had to be a coincidence. Soldiers from the Fire Realm didn't often come to Stoneham, but nothing about the fletcher's story implied the man would be the same one as in my dreams. Still, it couldn't hurt to get a look at him, just to ease my mind. I needed to head into the forest and bring back some game for Roark, but first I had to be sure.

I slipped into the back of the inn, where I found Tash and her mother Launa working in the kitchen, their eyes worried and their hands frantic, as if they needed to be doing something. Usually a clue that Roark was drinking again, although I didn't see any sign of him.

"Is everything all right?" I asked, as I removed my cloak and hung it by the door.

"There's a Fire Realm soldier in the tavern making everyone nervous." Tash tugged on her braid and gave me a concerned look. "And he's looking for someone who sounds a lot like you."

"Me?" I blinked. "What would a soldier want with me?"

"I don't know, but I don't like it."

"Perhaps you should hide," Launa said, her voice as soft as a dove's. "We'll tell him you left town."

I seriously considered it, or grabbing my things and running, like I should have done a month ago. But if this was the soldier I saw in my dreams, I had to meet him. It was the only way to find out more about this strange connection between us.

I touched Launa's arm gently. "I'll be okay."

She nodded, though her face was lined with concern. Tash gave me a hug and whispered for me to be careful, before I stepped out of the kitchen and into the tavern.

The soldier's back was to me, and the first thing I saw was his dark auburn hair, the same shade as it was in my dream. I swore my heart stopped beating as I took a step toward him, and then another. He must have heard me behind him, because he rose to his feet and turned around, his brown eyes meeting mine.

"You're her," he said.

Recognition slammed into me and I had a hard time speaking. Everything about him—from his perfectly tousled hair to his broad shoulders in a black and red military uniform—was familiar to me. I felt like I knew him already, even though we'd never met. But how was that possible?

How could this man from my dreams be standing in front of me?

And did that mean the other men were real as well?

4

JASIN

A month ago I'd been on patrol in the forest and had stopped to take a piss on a tree when the Fire God, in all his blazing glory, appeared out of thin air and told me to find a woman. And trust me, when a giant made out of flames tells you to do something, you do it. Especially when he wraps a scorching hand around your neck. Except instead of burning me alive, his power became absorbed into my body, branding me as the next Crimson Dragon.

The Fire God told me my duty and gave me a name—Kira—along with a split-second glimpse of her image and one month to find her. No directions. No hints. Not even a vague idea of what Realm she was in. Just an order to find her, serve her, and protect her. Then he vanished.

It took me a day or two to wrap my head around his demand and to believe it all really happened. The Fire God didn't just appear to people, especially ordinary guys like me. Don't get me wrong, I was a damn fine soldier, but that was it. Up until that point, I wasn't even sure the Gods were real. No one had heard from them in hundreds of years, after all. Now I'd been chosen by one of them to be his representative in this world and to take the place of the current Crimson Dragon, who wasn't going to be happy about being kicked out of the role.

I'd spent the last two weeks traveling from the Fire Realm, following the persistent urge that guided me north-west, into the farthest depths of the Earth Realm. Now the woman the Fire God sent me to find stood in front of me, and she was so gorgeous it made my blood heat like never before. Her shiny red hair was tied back in a tight ponytail, and I had the strongest urge to free it and let it fall about her shoulders. Her sharp eyes were an intriguing hazel color, as if many different shades danced within them. And her body, with those fit arms, full breasts, and curvy hips...damn. Maybe being tied to one woman for the rest of my life wouldn't be such a hardship after all.

A slow grin spread across my mouth. "I had no idea you'd be so beautiful in person. Thank the Gods indeed."

"Who are you?" Kira asked, with suspicion in her voice. She stared at me as if she recognized me, but wasn't sure how. Did she not know who I was? Or what *she* was?

"Name's Jasin," I said. "I've been sent to find you."

Her eyes narrowed. "Sent? By whom?"

"By the Fire God."

She took a step back and crashed into a chair, knocking

it to the ground, as fear and confusion crossed her face. "I don't understand."

Maybe she truly didn't know. Had she not been visited by the Spirit Goddess too? Did she not know about the task in front of us?

I glanced around, but the tavern was empty except for the two of us. I moved closer and lowered my voice anyway to be safe. "A few weeks ago I had a visit from the Fire God. He told me I was the future Crimson Dragon and that I had to find you—the next Black Dragon."

5

KIRA

Everyone knew the Black Dragon and the other Dragons were immortal. They'd ruled for the last thousand years, and would rule for another thousand to come. Each one was the divine representative of the five elemental Gods, hand-picked to serve them and reign over the rest of us. This man couldn't be one of them—and neither could I.

"No," I said, my head spinning. "Impossible."

"I'll prove it to you," the soldier—Jasin—said. He raised his hand and conjured a ball of flame, which danced across his fingertips.

Even with the heat from the fire, all I felt was cold terror. I turned on my heel and ran out of the inn as fast as I could while flashbacks of my parents' deaths filled my mind, their screams ringing in my ears even seven years later. There was no denying it anymore. Jasin truly was the

Crimson Dragon—and a soldier for the Onyx Army—which meant I had to get as far away from him as possible.

I dashed into the forest, down the hidden paths I knew like the back of my hand, crashing through the brush with my bow clutched tight in my fingers. I ran with only instinct and fear guiding me, without a firm plan in my mind other than to escape. Not just to save myself, but to save Tash and her mother too. I couldn't let him burn them alive, like the other Crimson Dragon had done to my family.

Jasin called out, "Wait!" He chased me into the forest, and with his long legs managed to catch up to me within minutes.

When I glanced back, he was almost upon me. I stumbled and tripped over a fallen tree and he crashed into me from behind, tumbling to the ground with me. We landed together with him on top, pinning me down with his hard, muscular body.

His face was close to mine and we were both breathing heavily, our chests pressed together. "I'm not going to hurt you," he said. "It's my duty to serve and protect you."

I stared into his eyes without backing down. "Why?"

"Because you're the Black Dragon."

I let out a sharp laugh. "Hardly."

"You are. Or you will be, once you've bonded with me and the other three Dragons. Then you'll be the strongest of us all."

The Black Dragon was the representative of the Spirit Goddess and could control all the elements. She always had four male Dragons as her mates, each one representing the different elements of fire, water, earth, and air. If Jasin was correct—which he obviously wasn't—then he would be one of the men bonded to me for life as my lover, my husband, and my guardian.

The idea of sleeping with the four men in my dreams sent a rush of desire between my legs, as did the feel of Jasin on top of me. With our eyes locked together, my lips parted and raging hot lust coursed through me. Sparks of passion seemed to flare between us, and for a second I gripped his shirt and nearly pulled his mouth down to mine.

Gods, what was wrong with me?

"Get off me," I said, shoving him aside before I did something stupid. I stood up and brushed the dirt and leaves off myself. "If you're right, then where are the other three?"

"I'm sure they'll be here soon. We were given your name and told we would bond with you in the order in which we arrived. Even if the others tried to ignore it, the need to find you became almost overwhelming as more days passed." He slowly stood as his dark eyes ran up and down my body like a caress. "I'm glad I was the first though."

I tried to ignore the way his suggestive smile made me as warm as the flame he'd conjured. "If you are the Crimson Dragon, then prove it. Shift into your other form."

"I can't. I've been chosen to be the next Crimson Dragon, but I won't become one truly until I bond with you in the Fire Temple. After that, you'll be able to control fire too and I'll be able to change into a dragon at will." He shrugged. "Or at least, that's what the Fire God told me."

"How convenient." I crossed my arms, skeptical of

everything he was telling me. Although he *had* summoned fire from thin air, so he wasn't completely full of lies. "You're a soldier in the Onyx Army. Why should I believe anything you say?"

All traces of amusement left his eyes and he looked away with a frown. "I was before, yes. Not anymore. I had to leave my post to find you and I can't ever return. They won't look kindly on a deserter."

No, they wouldn't. If the Onyx Army found him, they'd assume he was a traitor working with the Resistance and make an example of him. If he was telling the truth, of course. He was still wearing their uniform, after all, though his scaled armor was nowhere in sight.

I sighed as I debated what to do. I was still wary, but something told me to listen to him. Maybe because I already felt like I knew him after seeing him in my dreams for so many nights. Years of being on my own had made it hard for me to trust anyone, but Jasin felt familiar somehow. If nothing else, I should hear more of what he had to say.

"Let's head back to the inn and talk about this over some food," I finally said.

"There's nothing I would enjoy more." He gestured toward the inn. "Lead the way."

He kept pace with me easily, and as we walked we kept sneaking glances at each other. It was hard to believe he was real, and I wondered if he felt the same way. Not to mention, he was definitely easy on the eyes. All those muscles and that cocky smile...yeah, he must be popular with the ladies.

As we emerged from the forest, I spotted the stable boy bringing in a fine white horse with a saddle decorated with what looked like real gold. Other people who frequented the tavern were gawking at it, no doubt speculating about the nobleman it must belong to.

"Nice horse," Jasin said with suspicion, his hand resting on the pommel of his sword. "Wonder who the rider is."

I remembered my dream of the man in fine clothing reaching for a book. If what Jasin said was true, the nobleman I'd seen was likely the next Golden Dragon. Assuming any of this was real and not some kind of trick or con. I certainly didn't feel like the Black Dragon, and I had no magic of my own. All I had were strange dreams that had started when I'd been hit by lightning.

I stepped inside the inn with Jasin at my heels. Inside, the beautiful golden-haired man from my dream was chatting with Tash, who hung on his every word. He immediately turned toward me, as did everyone else in the tavern, but when our eyes met it was like we were the only people in the room. His face was perfectly sculpted with sharp cheekbones and intelligent eyes, and he possessed an elegance that set him apart from every other man I'd seen before in my life. My breath hitched and desire rushed through me like a hurricane, threatening to blow me away.

"You," he said, his voice full of awe.

6

AURIC

The woman who must be Kira stood before me clutching a bow in her hand, her eyes wide with surprise, but also something like recognition. She was so beautiful it made all other thoughts vanish from my mind, leaving only an intense curiosity about my future mate. I took a moment to study her, mentally logging everything including her worn boots, dark hunting leathers, wind-swept hair, and flushed cheeks. A single leaf was stuck to her brown cloak and, judging from her state, I guessed she had just come from the forest in a bit of a hurry.

Another man stood beside her wearing the black uniform of the Onyx Army, right down to a sword at his side. His eyes ran over me in a quick, suspicious appraisal. I held my breath, waiting for him to recognize me, but all he did was touch the pommel of his sword as he moved closer to Kira, silently warning me he would protect her with his life. He must be one of the other Dragons. One of the men I would have to share her with. But which one, I wondered?

"Who are you?" Kira asked me.

A tricky question indeed. I gazed around the tavern to take in the townsfolk who were all staring at us, including the cheerful waitress. They were intrigued by me, for sure, but no one gasped or shouted my name or kneeled before me. None of them realized who I truly was.

"Can we speak alone?" I asked Kira, keeping my voice low. I was sure she had a million questions, as did I. Questions that would be better answered without the entire town listening in.

She nodded, then turned to the waitress. "Tash, is the private dining room free?"

Tash's eyebrows practically shot through the roof as she glanced between me and Kira. "It's not booked tonight. Go on in and I'll bring you three something to eat." She brushed past Kira and said, "And you better tell me *everything* later."

"I will," Kira said.

She led us into a large room off the side of the tavern which was likely used for events, celebrations, or other private gatherings, containing one long wooden table and many chairs. A painting hung on the wall featuring the Black Dragon with her four consorts flying around her, surrounded by their representative element. Each one looked terrifying and powerful, with their scaled bodies, large wings, and long tails. I'd not seen this exact painting before, but the Black Dragon demanded that one like it had to be hung in any place where people gathered. No doubt it was to remind us that the five Dragons were watching over us at all times.

I gazed at the Golden Dragon in the painting and pondered my fate, while Kira closed the door behind us. I never would have believed any of this if the Air God himself hadn't granted me his powers. I still hardly believed it, even though my draw toward Kira was unmistakable.

She turned toward me, facing me down with uneasy eyes. "I think it's time you told me who you are and what you're doing here."

I hesitated, but I wasn't quite ready to reveal who I was yet. I wouldn't lie, but I wouldn't tell them the whole truth either. Not until I knew these people better. Not until I could trust them.

7

KIRA

T he golden-haired man stood up straighter, gazing
down at me from his towering height. "I'm Auric. I
was sent to find you by the Air God." He gave me a dramatic
bow, his movements refined and graceful. "I'm here to serve
the next Black Dragon."

Jasin snorted and muttered, "This guy? Really?"

I glared at him and turned back to Auric, sizing him up.
His traveling clothes were simple, yet nevertheless stood out
due to their fine quality and expensive fabrics. Auric was
definitely not from anywhere around here. A nobleman for
sure. He wasn't as obviously muscular as Jasin, but he was
just as handsome in a more refined way, with the most
amazing cheekbones I'd ever seen and gray eyes that
entranced me immediately. He looked at me as if I was the
answer to a problem he'd been trying to solve. I couldn't help

but be intrigued by him, especially after watching him in my dreams for a month.

"You said you had a visit from the Air God?" I asked.

He nodded. "Exactly one month ago."

"That's when I met the Fire God," Jasin said. A flame flickered idly across his fingers. "And when I got these powers."

That was the same day I turned twenty. The same night I'd been hit by lightning.

Gods, maybe it really was all true.

I dropped into a chair as it all finally sank in. If I was the Black Dragon, what did that mean exactly? There was only one Black Dragon, and she ruled our entire world. I somehow doubted she'd be thrilled about my presence. She was a cruel empress, and she definitely wasn't the type to share power. There was no way I could replace her. This all had to be some kind of mistake.

"Are you all right?" Auric asked, as he sat beside me, his voice concerned.

"Kira?" Jasin hovered behind me, his hands gripping the back of my chair protectively.

I looked into Auric's eyes, which were the color of storm clouds. "Show me."

For a second he seemed confused, but then realization dawned across his face. A breeze began to pick up in the room out of nowhere and soon grew into a strong wind that whipped my hair around my face, making me gasp.

The door opened and the magical wind instantly died.

Tash stepped inside, balancing three trays of food and drink with such skill it was almost like magic of her own. She set each one down while her eyes roamed over both men, and for a second I felt a flash of possessiveness. Which made me uncomfortable, because neither of these guys were mine, and I had no reason to feel anything but warmth toward Tash. Of course, if what these men said were true, then both of them were my future mates. Would I ever get used to the idea of that?

"Anything else you need?" Tash asked, while searching my face. Her concern for me shone through her warm eyes, and I knew she was asking if I was all right in here with these two strangers.

"We're all set, thank you," I told her with a smile that I hoped showed how grateful I was for her help. She was looking out for me, even if she had no idea what was going on.

She nodded and moved to leave the room, but was blocked by a huge, broad-shouldered man with muscular arms the size of tree trunks—the blacksmith I'd seen in my dreams. His eyes were a deep forest green, his skin was the color of tree bark, and his short beard gave him a rugged masculinity that was distinctly opposite Auric's elegant beauty and less refined than Jasin's handsome swagger. Yet I felt the same rush of desire, familiarity, and possessiveness when I looked at him as when I did the other two men.

Gods, what was wrong with me? I'd never felt this way about a single man before, yet now I felt it for *three* of them?

"Well, hello there," Tash said, staring at the new arrival with interest.

"I'm here to see Kira," the man said, his voice low and deep, like the rumble of an earthquake.

"Come inside," I said, with a nod to Tash.

As this new visitor stepped inside, Tash shook her head as if bewildered. She left us alone and shut the door, and suddenly the room seemed a lot smaller with the large mountain of a man inside.

"My name is Slade," he said, his intense eyes fixed on mine. "I've been looking for you, Kira."

"How do you know my name?" I asked him.

"The Earth God told me."

"Let me guess. He came to you a month ago, gave you powers, and sent you to find me?" When he nodded, I rubbed the bridge of my nose, so overwhelmed by it all I could hardly think straight. "That was my twentieth birthday. I was struck by lightning that night. After that I began to see all of you in my dreams."

"You knew we were coming, then?" Auric asked, his eyebrows darting up.

"No. I only caught quick flashes or vague glimpses. I didn't think any of you were real. Just figments of my imagination. I never expected you to actually turn up here. Or to tell me you're the next Dragons, whatever that means."

"We were drawn to you," Slade said. "We couldn't stay away. Even if we wanted to."

Those last words held a touch of sadness or perhaps bitterness, and I knew there had to be a story behind them. All three men had given up their entire lives because the Gods had given them a duty and told them I was the Black

Dragon. If it was true, they'd each been chosen to serve me, protect me, and love me—against their will.

I stared down at my food, but I wasn't hungry. My thoughts made my stomach churn, but I couldn't deny it any longer. All three of the men had been given powers by the Gods on the same night I'd been struck by lightning, and I'd seen them in my dreams ever since. The men could control the elements, and I was strangely attracted to all of them.

Maybe I really was the next Black Dragon.

8

SLADE

I pulled out a chair and sat across from my future mate, taking her in. She was certainly beautiful, with an inner strength in her hazel eyes that made my gaze want to linger on her. That would make this situation easier, at least. I had no intention of ever giving her my heart, but if I was forced to be with her for the rest of my life, it helped I found her pleasing to look at. But was she ready for what we had to do next? Were any of us, for that matter?

"So you're the future Jade Dragon?" the soldier asked me. "Show us what you can do."

I leaned back and crossed my arms. "These powers were given to us by the Gods so we can protect people. Not to use idly."

He scoffed. "What's the point of having them if you can't have a little fun now and then?"

"Sorry, but I have to agree with Slade on this one," the

nobleman said. "Our powers should be used wisely, although we need to practice with them too, of course. We can enjoy that part, at least. I'm Auric, by the way."

"Jasin," the soldier said.

So these were two of the men I'd be sharing my mate with. I shook my head at their youthful eagerness. They sat closely on either side of Kira, as if already staking their claim on her. The soldier in particular seemed impatient and overly excited, especially the way he was constantly moving, like he was full of energy he couldn't contain. The nobleman was calmer but had his head in the clouds, as evidenced when he pulled out a journal and began jotting down notes. Kira simply watched us all as though she couldn't believe her eyes. I didn't blame her.

I had probably ten years or more on all of the people at this table. It made sense that they were chosen—they were in the prime of their lives and ready to go on adventures, full of idealism and big dreams of saving the world. They likely had nothing tying them down either. Not me though. I'd already tried to help save the world and gave up on that task. Back home I had a good, stable life, one I wasn't ready to leave behind. Why had the Earth God chosen me instead of someone else? How could he expect me to just abandon everything I'd spent my entire life building up?

After he visited me, I'd struggled with my new destiny. I'd always been devoted to the Gods, and one couldn't simply turn down new powers and a divine mission. But I'd waited as long as I could to leave my home and travel here, even though it was only a day's ride away. If not for the nagging feeling in my gut, I might not have left at all.

I didn't ask for this. I didn't want this. I still wasn't sure I was the right person for the role of Jade Dragon. But even with all my doubts, I was here and I was fully committed to our mission. I would do whatever it took to serve the Gods and protect Kira.

It was my duty, after all.

9

KIRA

After Tash brought Slade a tray of food, all three men dove in while I studied them. They were each so different, yet I felt a strange connection to all of them. But there was one more man in my dreams, who must be the future Azure Dragon. Where was he now?

I took a long breath. "Okay, assuming this is all true and we are the next Dragons—which I'm not sure I believe yet—what does that mean? Why do the Gods even need another set of Dragons?"

"We're meant to overthrow the current Dragons and take their place as the protectors of the world," Auric said, his voice rather matter-of-fact considering he was talking treason.

My jaw fell open and it took a moment for me to speak. "What?"

"That's what I was told as well," Slade said.

"But why?" I asked.

Jasin shrugged casually. "Sounds like the Gods aren't happy with the way the Black Dragon and her men are ruling the world." He picked up a grape and popped it in his mouth. "Time for a change in leadership."

"Maybe they've chosen us to set things right," Slade said.

All of the men were being way too calm about this, considering what they were saying. Then again, they'd had a month to get used to the idea. Even so, I could barely wrap my mind around it. The Gods had been nothing but myth for so long that most people had stopped believing they were real at all. If the men were telling the truth—and I was starting to believe they might be—then perhaps the Gods had finally awoken and were doing something to help their people for a change. We certainly needed it.

But why me? I was a nobody. Definitely not a hero, and certainly not the kind of person who could overthrow the Black Dragon and her men. They'd ruled for thousands of years and were the most powerful beings in the world—how were we supposed to stop them?

"What are we meant to do?" I finally asked.

Auric set his fork down and met my gaze. "We must travel to each of the Gods' temples, visiting them in the order in which we arrived today. There you will have to bond with one of us, which will unlock our full powers and the dragon form. You will gain our powers as well, and once you've bonded with all of us, you'll visit the Spirit Goddess's temple to become the Black Dragon. After that, we should be strong enough to face the current Dragons."

My head spun, trying to process everything he said. "What do you mean, bonded?"

"Err..." Auric shifted in his seat a little. "You would officially take us as your mate in the most...intimate way."

Jasin flashed me a naughty grin. "What he means is that we need to have sex." He leaned back in his chair with his arms folded behind his head. "Not sure about you guys, but I for one am looking forward to all of this."

"Of course you are," I said, rolling my eyes, even as heat flared inside me at the thought of becoming intimate with all of them. "Don't get too excited, because I haven't agreed to any of this." I turned back to Auric. "So all we have to do is travel to the temples and uh, bond with each other?"

"Exactly."

I arched an eyebrow. "You seem to know a lot about this."

Auric shrugged as a small smile touched his lips. "The Air God told me some of it. The rest I learned after doing some research before I came here, although I couldn't find much information overall. I suspect if books about this ever did exist, the Black Dragon had most of that knowledge purged. I'm hoping we can uncover more on this journey."

"You make all of this sound so easy," Slade said, as his long fingers rubbed his dark beard. "What happens when the Black Dragon and the others find out about us?"

"Good point," I said. "I have a hard time seeing any of the Dragons giving up their powers willingly."

"We'll try to travel without attracting attention," Jasin said. "Keep our powers and our mission secret for as long as we can. But we should leave first thing in the morning."

"What about the last member of our team?" Slade asked.

Jasin shrugged. "He'll catch up. It's his problem he wasn't here on time."

"The Gods *did* tell us to be here in exactly one month," Auric said, his brow furrowing.

They wanted to leave tomorrow? I'd wanted to run, but not yet, and not like this. Certainly not with three complete strangers. "We're not going anywhere," I said, rising to my feet. "Not until we know more about what is going on here and what we're supposed to do next."

All three men looked like they might argue with me, but I shot them a fierce look and headed for the door. I needed some space, needed to get away from them and everything they represented. Maybe they were destined to be bonded to me, but they weren't my mates yet. I didn't know a damn thing about them, I hadn't chosen them, and I certainly wasn't going off on some dangerous quest with them.

I found Tash in the kitchen, stirring a stew with a long ladle. As soon as I entered, she spun around. "What's going on? Who are those men? Why are they here?"

Her rapid words made my head spin even more, but I had to tell someone what was going on to make sure I wasn't dreaming. I grabbed her arm and dragged her into my bedroom, then shut the door. "I'll tell you everything, but I warn you now, it barely makes sense to me."

She sat on the edge of the bed, leaning forward anxiously. "Maybe we can sort through it together."

"According to those guys, they're Dragons. Or they will be." It sounded even more ridiculous when I said it out loud. "But they already have magic."

Her brow furrowed. "How is that possible? The Dragons are immortal and there are only five of them. How does someone *become* one?"

"I don't know. But each man says one of the Gods chose him, gave him magic, and then told him to find me."

"I've never heard of such a thing." She tilted her head and frowned. "Please don't take this the wrong way, because you know I love you like a sister...but why you?"

I drew in a long breath. "Supposedly I'm the next Black Dragon."

She gasped. "What?"

"Trust me, I'm as shocked as you are." I ran my fingers through my long hair, where they got caught on the tangled ends. "Do you remember on my birthday when I came inside all muddy?"

"Of course."

"Right before that I was struck by lightning, but it didn't hurt me at all. Ever since then I've had these weird dreams of four men with elemental powers. Three of those men are now sitting in the other room, and I'm guessing the fourth will be here soon. I'm supposed to go with them to each of the Gods' temples now to 'bond' with them—and after that we'll be the next Dragons. Which I'm pretty sure the current Dragons won't be thrilled about. Especially when they learn we're supposed to overthrow them."

She stared at me as if she'd never seen me before. "Are you going to do it?"

I paced back and forth in front of her. "No way. I don't know a thing about those men. I'm not sure I believe any of this is real, anyway. It sounds even crazier now that I've said it all out loud. There must be some other explanation..."

She chewed on her lower lip as she considered. "I think you should do it."

I stopped and gawked at her. "What?"

"If any of it is true, then you have a chance to change things. You've been chosen by the Gods to make this world better and stop the Black Dragon's reign." A mischievous look entered her eyes. "Plus it means you'll be married to four very handsome men. It's hard to complain about that."

I sank onto the bed beside her and buried my face in my hands. "But I didn't ask for any of this! I don't want to change things or to go up against the Black Dragon. I just want to live a quiet, peaceful life and stay out of trouble. And I don't want four men, or even one." That wasn't exactly true, but the whole thing was far too overwhelming for me to even consider what being married to four men would mean.

She rubbed my back slowly. "It seems that's not what the Gods have in mind for you. They've chosen you, Kira. You have to answer their call."

"Curse the Gods," I muttered, then immediately regretted it. Were they watching me even now? Would they strike me with lightning again if I didn't do what they wanted?

The door suddenly burst open, and at first I thought it was the Gods coming to punish me. But it was no God, only Tash's father, who was almost as terrifying.

Roark stood in the doorway, his large hulking form completely filling it, as he glared at us. "There you are."

10

KIRA

Roark quickly took us both in with disgust written across his face. "What do you think you're doing? Lazing about while we have customers waiting! Get back to work!"

Tash scrambled to her feet. "I was only taking a short break, Father."

He grunted, then narrowed his eyes at me. "And you. It's been two days since you last brought us any game." He pointed to the door. "I have hungry soldiers out there demanding some supper. What am I supposed to tell them?"

Dread and panic shot through my blood. I'd been on my way to the forest to hunt when Jasin had shown up. "I'll go right now. I'll find something quickly, I promise."

"Too late for that." A sick grin twisted his lips as he grabbed Tash's shoulder, his meaty fingers digging into her dress until she cried out. "You know what the punishment is for slacking off."

"Father, please," Tash started, but then was cut off when he backhanded her across the face.

"Stop," I pleaded. "I'll get you whatever you want right now. Just don't hurt her."

"The two of you siting here gossiping while the rest of us starve," he growled, before striking Tash again. "You both need to be taught a lesson."

"No!" I yelled, then launched myself at him. He was double my size if not more—as well as being both my employer and my landlord—but I couldn't let him hurt my best friend. Not again.

I tore at him with my nails, reaching for whatever I could, caught in an urgent frenzy to protect Tash. With a roar, he threw me off him in a burst of strength. I fell back, my head slamming hard on the wall behind me, before slumping to the floor in a daze of pain and darkness. *Tash, I'm sorry.*

When the black haze lifted, three silhouettes stood in the doorway.

A flash of fire danced before my eyes. A rumble shook through my bones. A burst of wind tore at my hair. Roark was thrown across the room, knocked to his knees, and surrounded by flames. My three mates moved around him, their faces filled with disgust and rage.

"You will not hurt either of these ladies again," Slade said, his voice low and foreboding.

Roark looked up at the men standing around him with

both fear and hatred. "I can do what I want in my own inn. To my own women."

"Not anymore," Jasin said. The circle of flames grew hotter and danced around Roark, who yelped and shied back from it.

"Swear you won't touch them in violence again," Auric said, his voice as commanding as a prince's. "Swear on the Gods. And believe me, they're listening."

"I swear it," Roark bit out, but his eyes were full of menace.

The flames vanished. "Get out of here," Jasin said.

Roark scrambled to his feet and bolted from the room like it was still on fire. Although he seemed afraid, I doubted he would heed their warning. He would come for Tash again—he always did.

Slade knelt beside me and asked, "Are you all right?"

I nodded, though my throat was so dry I could barely speak. "Tash?"

"I'm here," she said, from behind Jasin. "I'm okay."

"Thank the Gods," I whispered, as I grabbed Slade's hand and rose to my feet. I swayed a little as a rush of pain threatened to knock me to the floor again, but he wrapped a comforting arm around me and held me steady. For a second I was distracted by his broad chest and strong arms, overcome with the urge to lean into him and let him hold me some more. He smelled good too, with an earthy, pine scent that reminded me of the forest in the morning. I took a deep breath to ground myself before pulling away from him.

"Thanks for the help, but I could have handled it," I said, as I rubbed the back of my aching head.

"He hurt you," Slade said gruffly, as if that explained everything.

"We're bound to protect you," Auric added.

"Thanks," I muttered. "And now you've cost me my job and my home, no doubt."

Jasin sheathed his sword. "We need to head out in the morning anyway."

I ignored him and moved to Tash, checking her face for injury. "Are you truly okay?"

"Yes, he didn't hit me that hard," she said, as she ran a hand over her jaw.

I glanced between her and the three men, torn between staying and leaving. Between my old, familiar life and an unknown, new one. Both seemed far too dangerous for my liking. I had no desire to leave, but after what they'd done to Roark, I couldn't exactly stay here anymore either. But who would protect Tash and make sure the inn had enough food?

"We'll talk more about this in the morning," I told the three men. "I need some time and space to gather my thoughts."

Tash wrung her hands as she addressed them. "You'll have to stay somewhere else, unfortunately. My father owns this inn."

"You sure we can't sleep in here?," Jasin asked, his eyes gleaming. "For Kira's protection of course."

"Good idea," Slade said, with a sharp nod.

"Not a chance," I said. "Like Tash said, it's better if you don't stay in this inn. I'll be fine. He won't bother me again tonight." Unless he got really drunk, anyway.

"Very well, but we'll be nearby if you need us," Auric said.

"I'll find you all someone else to board with," Tash said, leading the men out of my bedroom. They followed her reluctantly, each one glancing back at me with emotions in their eyes. Curiosity. Protectiveness. Desire.

As soon as they were gone, I changed my clothes and crumpled onto the bed, my head pounding. I had a lot to think about, but Roark must have hit me harder than I thought, because my eyes kept closing, and soon sleep carried me away.

I awoke to the sound of the door creaking open and instantly tensed, reaching for the knife I always kept under my pillow. My bedroom was completely dark except for the dim moonlight coming through the windows, which revealed two tall figures creeping into my bedroom. Fear made me immediately alert, but I held my breath and waited. I recognized Roark's broad profile and guessed the other man was his drinking buddy, Koth. Each of them reeked of alcohol, making my nose burn.

This time, my dream men couldn't save me. I was on my own.

"You're going to pay," Roark said. He reached for me, but I slashed at him with my dagger. He jerked back with a howl as it sliced through his arm, and then I pivoted on the bed, turning to ward off my next attacker. I was better with a bow, but I'd been taught a few fighting moves while living for a short time with some bandits. I hadn't fought in years, but luckily my body seemed to remember what to do.

Koth dodged my attack, while Roark grabbed my arms tightly from behind. I struggled, lashing out with my feet, as he dragged me back toward him.

"Let me go!" I yelled.

"Where are your friends now?" Roark asked, his breath hot at my ear. He tossed me to the ground hard, then moved to kick me. I tucked my arms and rolled out of the way, gripping my knife tightly. I swiped at his leg and he danced back, but I took that second to get to my feet and bolt from the room.

I ran through the dark kitchen as fast as I could, clutching my dagger in my shaking hand. Heavy footsteps pounded behind me as I reached the door leading outside, but before I could open it, someone struck me on the back of my head.

I fell against the door, momentarily dazed, even as my brain screamed at me to run and fight. Through the haze I managed to spin around and knee Roark between the legs, but Koth was there too.

His blow got me hard, right in the stomach. All the air left me in a swift whoosh and was replaced by lancing pain. Stars danced across my vision, but I wouldn't let my life end, not like this.

I stabbed the dagger into Koth's chest with one last burst of strength. Koth howled as I buried the knife deep in him, and then he hit the floor. But I wasn't safe yet.

"What have you done?" Roark asked, as he stared at his friend. When he took a step toward me, I wasn't sure how I could stop him. Not when he looked at me with murder in his eyes.

A thin knife flew across the room and landed in the wall beside Roark with a sharp *thunk*. A dark figure in a black hooded cloak stood on the other side of the kitchen, with a sword in one hand. A matching sword hung from his waist.

"Get away from her," the cloaked man said, his voice like ice.

"This is none of your concern, stranger," Roark said, glaring at him.

"I'm making it my concern."

Roark ignored the man and grabbed my arm, yanking me toward him. A blade flashed, glinting in the moonlight. A gurgling choke came from Roark's mouth. Blood sprayed across my dress.

Roark let me go and fell to the floor, his throat slashed by the cloaked man who now stood behind him. I hadn't even heard him move.

I gaped at my strange rescuer, wondering if I should be thankful or fearful. "Who are you?"

"Reven." He held up his blade and the blood flew off it in a magical swirl before he sheathed the sword. As he turned toward me, I caught a flash of dangerous blue eyes and a sharp jaw traced with dark stubble from under his hood. Familiarity crept through me and I realized who he was.

The last of my four mates had arrived.

11

REVEN

Walking in on the woman I'd been sent to find being attacked wasn't what I'd expected this evening, but it also wasn't all that uncommon in my line of work.

"Are you hurt?" I asked her, while I checked the area to make sure there were no other attackers.

She rubbed the back of her head. "A little banged up, but otherwise fine. Thanks to you."

I examined the two men on the floor—the one I'd killed, and the one with a dagger sticking out of his chest, presumably Kira's. I yanked it out, used my magic to remove the blood from the blade, then handed it to her. "Who were they?"

"Drunken fools who enjoyed hurting women," she muttered. "Problem is, one of them owns this place. Or he did, anyway."

Footsteps sounded behind us and I reached for one of

my swords again, but it was only a young woman in a chemise. She paused in the doorway and gasped when she saw the bodies on the floor.

"Father?" she asked, with a slight sob.

"I'm so sorry, Tash," Kira said. "Koth and your father attacked me while I was asleep. I didn't mean for this to happen."

Another older woman ran into the room, and she let out a strangled gasp at the sight of the dead men. The other woman, Tash, was already crying, and the two women collapsed into each other's arms with a sob. Kira watched with sympathy, while I took the chance to admire her. Despite being forced into this against my will, I had to admit she was pretty easy on the eyes. Her red hair was lightly mussed and her cheeks were flushed from the attack. Her thin chemise hugged her body in ways that awakened parts of me I usually tried to ignore. She was obviously brave and quite capable, since she'd killed one of the men before I'd intervened. But none of that mattered, because I was getting out of this mess as quickly as possible.

Kira gestured for me to follow her while we left the sobbing women in the kitchen. We stepped into a back room with a small bed, which she sank onto as she covered her face with her hands. She took a long breath, then looked up at me again. "I'm assuming you're here because you're the next Azure Dragon."

"Something like that," I said, with obvious distaste.

"I get the feeling you're not pleased about that."

That was an understatement. "I'm here, aren't I?"

"Yes, you are. And a good thing too, because it seems it's time I left this town." She began pulling clothes out of a wardrobe and packing them in a bag, while I crossed my arms and leaned against the doorway.

"I assume the others are already here then," I said.

"Yes, they're staying somewhere else. It's a long story." She sighed as she shoved a pair of ragged-looking slippers in the bag. "A few hours ago I led a quiet life. Now two men are dead and four men say I have to bond with them and become a Dragon. Why is this happening to me?"

I didn't reply. It had taken me a long time to accept that the Water God had truly chosen me. I'd ignored it at first. Then I'd gotten angry. Eventually I'd tried yelling, bargaining, and even praying to get out of it. I hated the Black Dragon and her mates with every fiber of my being, but that didn't mean I wanted to get involved in some mad quest that would only end up with all of us getting killed. But no matter how much I resisted, I couldn't deny the tugging in my gut that got worse with every day that passed, until the need to find Kira became all-encompassing. So here I was.

But as soon as I could find a way to get out of this mess, I was gone.

12

KIRA

I didn't get any more sleep that night. After telling my
story to the town's soldiers and trying to comfort Tash
and her mother, I'd accepted it was time for me to say my
goodbyes. It was clear I couldn't stay here any longer, no
matter how hard it was to leave my home behind.

Roark and Koth had never been especially loved in
Stoneham, but they were respected. They'd lived in the
town their entire lives and were related to half the people in
it. The soldiers believed me when I'd said their deaths were
a result of self-defense, especially when Tash and her
mother backed up my story, but the townspeople would
never look at me the same way again. Especially if word got
out about my new companions' strange magic. So far no one
else knew about them, but how long would that last?

No, the longer we stayed, the more dangerous it was for
everyone. Including Tash.

"Are you sure you'll be okay?" I asked her for the tenth time. We stood in the middle of her kitchen, with dawn's light filtering through the windows and illuminating the shadows under her eyes. Tash hadn't slept much either last night.

"I'm sure," she said, with a weak smile. Her eyes were puffy and red, but she stood tall, as if a great burden had lifted from her shoulders. "We both knew something like this would happen eventually. I'm only grateful none of us were hurt."

I took her hands in mine. "I'm sorry. I'm so sorry."

"It's all right." She squeezed my hands. "You protected me for so long, and my mother too. But it had to end some-day. At least now we can live without fear, and you can fulfill your destiny without worrying about me anymore."

"I hate leaving you behind," I said. "You could come with us, you know."

She chuckled softly. "What, and travel the world with you and your four men to help overthrow the Black Dragon? That sounds fun, but my place is here. I have an inn to run, after all."

I nodded. I knew that would be her answer, but I had to ask anyway. "You're going to be amazing at it. But what about food?"

"I'm reaching out to the farmers my father made angry to see if they'll do business with me instead." A sad smile touched her lips. "Don't worry about me, I'll figure it out. Just make sure you come back and visit sometime, okay? I want to hear all about your adventures."

"I will, I promise."

"And be careful." She gave me a tight hug. "I believe in you, Kira. If anyone can save this world, it's you."

Emotion made my throat tight as I hugged her back. "I'll do my best."

We said one last tearful goodbye and then I rushed out the kitchen door and headed toward the stables. I lifted my pack up on my shoulder while wiping my eyes before approaching the four men who waited for me near their horses. The four men I was supposed to spend the rest of my life with. Starting now.

Gods, I was not ready for this at all.

Reven leaned against the stable walls with his arms crossed, his hood pulled low over his face so all I could see was his dark stubble. He'd barely said a word to the other men, so it wasn't just me he was chilly with. I got the feeling he wasn't all that excited about being here, and how could I blame him? We'd all been forced into this situation, but there was nothing to do except make the best of it somehow —and trust that the Gods had chosen us for a reason.

The other men stood apart from each other as well. Jasin rocked on his heels, his fingers resting on the hilt of his sword as if he might pull it out at any moment, while he watched for any trouble from the soldiers or other townspeople. He wore his military uniform again, which consisted of black trousers with a stiff coat over them, both trimmed with dark red to show he was from the Fire Realm division. As a former member of the Onyx Army, could I really trust him?

Slade stood inside the stables, saddling a large brown horse with gentle eyes. He had a calm way about him, perhaps because he was a few years older than the rest of us. I had no doubt he was loyal to our cause, and I couldn't forget the way it had felt to be held in his arms for even a brief moment, but I had the sense something was holding him back too.

Auric peered at a map and took notes in his journal while the wind tousled his golden hair. His clothes were finer than the rest of ours and I wondered how he felt about being stuck with a girl like me, so below his station. I got the feeling he saw our mission as a chance to uncover hidden knowledge, but was that all he cared about? Could he ever care about me?

Would any of these men?

Not Reven, for sure. Slade was just as distant. Jasin maybe, though I got the feeling he'd be willing to bond with just about any woman.

"We need to make a plan," Auric said, snapping me out of my thoughts.

I drew in a breath as I stared at his map, which was more elaborate and finely made than any I'd seen before. Done in different colors, it depicted the four Realms, each one converging in the center at the capital, Soulspire, where the Black Dragon and her mates resided near the Spirit Temple. The Earth Realm, where we were now, was located in the north, with the Air Realm to the east, the Water Realm to the west, and the Fire Realm to the south. The map had each Realm's capital labelled, along with some other major cities, rivers, lakes, mountain ranges, and—most importantly —the five Gods' temples.

"We have to visit the temples in the order in which we arrived," Auric said. "That means the Fire Temple is first."

"Why can't we go to the Air or Earth one first?" I asked. "They're both closer."

"Because that's what the Gods decreed," Slade said.

Jasin flashed me a suggestive grin. "Definitely fine with me."

"I suspect they made that rule to keep it fair and to encourage us to find you faster," Auric said, with a shrug. "Either way, we need to head to the Fire Realm first."

For the next few minutes, Auric, Jasin, and I plotted a course to the Fire Temple, with a few helpful comments from Slade, while Reven ignored us entirely. Once that was done, the men's horses were brought out, each one as unique as their riders. I didn't have a horse, and certainly didn't have the money to buy one. Not that there were any for sale in a town as small as Stoneham anyway.

"You'll have to take turns riding with one of us," Auric said, from atop his elegant white horse with the gold-trimmed saddle.

"She can ride me any time." Jasin winked. "I mean, ride *with* me."

"I'm sure that's what you meant." I rolled my eyes and threw my pack on the back of Auric's horse. Jasin was a little too eager, and the other two were keeping their distance from me, so Auric it was.

Auric offered me his hand and I climbed onto the horse

behind him. A jolt of surprise and desire shot through me when I pressed against his back, along with the realization of how close we were. It had been years since I'd been this close to a man, but in the next few days I'd have to sit with all of the men like this. Of course, if they were really my mates, I'd be doing a lot more than just riding a horse with them soon.

I hesitated, then slid my arms around Auric, trying not to focus on the feel of his strong chest or his clean, fresh scent that made me want to get even closer. He sucked in a breath at my touch, but then rested his hand over mine and gave it a quick squeeze.

"Ready?" he asked.

I cast one last glance back at the town that had been my home for the last three years, then turned to gaze at my other companions. Each one was staring at me, waiting for me to give the signal to leave. Reven, on his swift black steed, looking broody and bored. Jasin, impatiently twitching on his dark stallion that looked like it was no stranger to combat. And Slade, on his large chocolate brown horse, waiting with a steady, calm demeanor.

"Let's go," I said.

My arms tightened around Auric as the horse began to move. It had been three years since I'd ridden a horse and I had the feeling it would take some time to get used to it again. By the time we stopped, I'd probably be sore all over.

As we rode out of town, the soldiers watched us with stony glares and a few people stepped out of their houses to gawk at our strange procession, but no one seemed all that sad to see me leave. I'd killed Koth, and might as well have killed Roark too. They weren't the first men I'd killed and likely wouldn't be the last, but their deaths still weighed heavily on me. Taking a life never got easier, nor did seeing a dead body, even if the person deserved it. I only hoped Tash and her mother would be okay.

I gazed at the forest where I'd gone hunting every day for the last few years. I'd promised Tash I would return someday, but it was hard to know what lay ahead of me, or how different I would be if I did return. Would I truly be the Black Dragon then? I'd never seen the current Black Dragon before, but I knew she was immortal, could control all four elements, and turned into a great winged beast with huge talons and glowing eyes. Was that my fate as well?

And what would the Black Dragon do when she learned I was like her?

13

AURIC

Kira was quiet as we left Stoneham and traveled on the road alongside the edge of the forest, but I was constantly aware of her presence. Not only were her arms wrapped tight around my chest, but her feminine curves were pressed against my back in a way that was hard to ignore. Especially since I wasn't used to anything like this. I spent my time with books and...well, that was about it. I certainly wasn't very good with women and didn't know what to say to them. Now I was put in a position where I desperately wanted to get to know my future mate better, but was also unsure how to talk to her. I bet none of the other men had that problem.

"Is your head okay?" I asked her.

She pressed a hand to the back of her head. "Surprisingly it is. No pain at all, actually. They must not have hit me as hard as I'd thought."

"That's good." I paused. "Are you comfortable?"

"As comfortable as can be expected, considering I haven't ridden a horse in years." She shifted behind me, making her breasts rub against my back, a sensation that made my trousers suddenly tight. "How long do you think it will take to reach the Fire Temple?"

"I estimate it will take about eight or nine days, depending on how long we stop and if we have to go out of our way to avoid any problems."

"Is that all?" she asked, her voice hollow.

Was she nervous about this too? "I believe we've mapped out the most efficient route, but if you'd like to go slower or stop somewhere along the way I'm sure it won't be a problem."

"No, it's fine," she said, then drew in a long breath. "Eight or nine days is simply not a lot of time to get to know all of you, before we..."

"Before we become mates."

"Yes."

I understood her concern all too well. "None of us want to rush you. Take as much time as you need." I hesitated, glancing over at the Fire Realm soldier, who looked at ease on his horse. "You might want to spend extra time with Jasin though, since you'll have to bond with him first."

"Probably. But your temple is second."

"True." I cleared my throat at the thought of what that meant. "You'll have a lot more time to get to know Slade and Reven before we arrive at their temples, at least."

"I suppose so," she said. "What else can you tell me about all of this?"

"Not much, I'm afraid. I scoured the library in Stormhaven for any information after the Air God visited me, but found very little of interest. What I did find, I picked up from various different texts that otherwise seemed to have nothing to do with the Black Dragon or the Gods. One was on geography, one was on fashion, and one was on food. I suspect the Black Dragon had the rest destroyed."

"Probably," Kira said. "She didn't want anyone to be able to challenge her."

"That seems likely. I'm hoping I might be able to uncover more during our travels. I'd like to record all of this too, for future generations. Assuming we survive and the Black Dragon doesn't destroy my writings too."

"So you're a scholar?" she asked. "And a nobleman, I assume, judging from your clothes."

I tried not to react to her question and chose my words carefully. "Yes, I'm a member of House Killian, but I spend most of my days in the library. Or I did before all of this, anyway."

"House Killian? Does that mean you're related to the royal family of the Air Realm?"

"Yes," I replied hesitantly. I didn't want to lie to her, but I didn't feel comfortable divulging the full story yet. "But I'm no one of consequence." There, that was true enough.

"Maybe not to you, but I guarantee your life has been very different from mine and the other men. You grew up in luxury and never had to worry about where your next meal would come from or whether you could afford to repair your shoes."

I wondered what she had gone through before we arrived in her village. She wasn't wrong either. Gods, she must think I was pathetic, and if she only knew the full truth, she'd definitely think the worst of me. Now I really couldn't tell her. "That is true. I grew up in privilege and have little to complain about."

"I didn't mean what I said as an insult," Kira added, with the slightest brush of her hand against mine. "I was only pointing out the differences between all of us."

"I understand." I tilted my head as I considered. "Perhaps the Gods chose the four of us to be your mates for the sheer reason that we *are* all so different from one another."

"That could be. The Air God didn't give you any hint of why he picked you?"

"No, not at all. He was pretty vague about everything though. Of course, I was also pretty shocked at the time, so I didn't get to ask him as many questions as I would have liked."

"What happened? I know you all supposedly met the Gods, but I don't know the details."

My hands tightened on the reins as I thought back to what occurred a month ago. "I've always been an early riser, and I like to take breakfast outside in the garden at dawn, usually with a book or two. That morning it was unusually windy outside and I could barely read because the pages kept turning. I nearly went inside, but then he appeared. The Air God."

"What did he look like?" she asked.

"Like a giant made out of a tornado. He was composed of swirling wind and lightning, and his voice was like thunder. As he spoke to me, everything around me floated in the air. My books. My breakfast. The bench I'd been sitting on." I shook my head, remembering how shocked and confused I'd been. "He told me I'd been chosen to be the next Golden Dragon and that I had to find you so we could take the place of the current Dragons. Then he sent a rush of air through me, lifting me up into the sky, and I thought I would surely plummet to my death. Instead I floated back down, but he was gone."

"It sounds like something from a dream."

"Yes, it does. I questioned everything that happened, sure that I'd been imagining it all, but then I began moving things without touching them, and one night woke up floating in the air. Not to mention, I had this overwhelming urge to head northwest to find you."

"What did your family think of all that?" she asked.

"I didn't tell them anything. The Air God warned me not to speak of this with anyone except you and your other mates. Of course, it was difficult to hide my powers from my family, but people are often willing to believe there was a sudden gust of wind or a strange breeze instead of magic."

"Were they okay with you leaving?"

"I informed them I was traveling to Thundercrest to visit the library there, but once I was on the road I escaped my guards and came here." I frowned as my guilt at deceiving my family returned. "I left them a note telling them I was all right, but they're probably looking for me now. I hope they're not too worried."

She shifted again behind me, as if trying to get comfortable. "Are you close with your family?"

"Yes. For the most part." Talking about my family would be tricky without revealing more about who I truly was, so I changed the subject. "What of you? I'm guessing those people back there were not your family."

"No, my family is long gone."

I heard something in her voice that made me think this wasn't something she cared to elaborate on, and I fell silent. I could understand not wanting to talk about some things about our pasts. None of that mattered anyway. Our old lives were over. What mattered now was the journey ahead of us.

14

KIRA

We traveled along the road with the forest all around us, Jasin in the lead to make sure the way was clear, while Slade and Reven rode behind to guard our backs. On any other day I would be heading into the forest right now and trying to find some game for Roark to make sure that Tash would be safe and that I would be fed tonight. Now I was sitting behind this man I'd just met, with three other strange men around me, and together we were supposed to save the world. I still didn't know how I had gotten involved in this, and wondered if it was all a big mistake. Maybe the men were supposed to find some other girl. Maybe the Gods chose wrong.

Even if I ignored the whole "overthrow the Black Dragon" goal, which was so far-fetched it was laughable, the thought of bonding with all the men was hard to swallow. We would be mated for the rest of our lives, with the four of them sharing me forever. It was hard to believe they would be okay with that. I could barely fathom it myself, although I had to admit I didn't hate the idea either. I had to give the Gods credit, they'd certainly found me four men who made my mouth water.

I supposed the only thing to do now was to get to know my future mates better. I'd made some progress with Auric, and over the next few days I'd learn what I could about the other men as well. Especially Jasin. In less than two weeks I'd be expected to sleep with him, and I barely knew a thing about him.

At midday, we stopped beside a small stream for a break and to have a quick meal, but none of us felt like chatting much. I intended to ride with Jasin next, but then I caught him casting fire, moving it from hand to hand like a juggling ball, and fear crept down my spine. Even though he wasn't the one who'd killed my family, I'd had a fear of fire ever since that day.

I decided to ride with Slade, whose solid, quiet presence soothed me as we rode east through the Earth Realm. He was so large and muscular it was a pleasure to hold onto him and feel all that contained strength under my arms, even if he had no interest in making conversation.

When the sun touched the horizon, Jasin called for us to halt. "This looks like a good place to camp for the evening."

He'd chosen a spot in a small clearing near a freshwater stream. Thick trees sheltered us on either side, filled with the sounds of birds chirping as they found their resting spots for the night.

As I eased off Slade's horse, I let out a pained groan. Every muscle in my body seemed to hurt, especially my thighs and back. If I was this sore after only a few hours of riding, how would I make it through nine or ten days of this?

"Are you all right?" Slade asked, resting one of his large hands lightly on my shoulder.

I stretched my back, trying to ease the aches in it. "Just sore. I haven't ridden in some time."

"You'll get used to it," Jasin said. "I've seen plenty of soldiers get broken in. Try to stretch and walk around, that will help."

"Sitting behind one of us can't be helping either," Slade said.

Jasin nodded. "We should get her a horse when we can."

"With what money?" I asked.

"Money isn't an issue," Auric said.

I blew out a long breath. "Maybe not at the moment, but we have a long journey ahead of us."

Reven stayed silent the entire time, almost as if he wasn't there at all. He removed his things from his horse, then spread his bedroll out on one side of the clearing. The rest of us followed his lead, quickly setting up camp while the sky darkened.

I grabbed my bow and headed into the forest before the men could stop me. Tash's mother had been kind enough to pack us some rations, but they would only last so long if we didn't supplement them with fresh food. Besides, we would need to keep our energy up for the journey ahead. We could stop in an inn every few days, but that wasn't possible every night.

The Spirit Goddess must have been smiling upon me, because I managed to take down a large gray hare almost immediately. Maybe she had chosen me after all, although I didn't remember a visit from her.

Wait. The old woman I'd found in the forest. Could that have been her? If so, why hadn't she given me more information? Or some powers, like the guys had gotten from their Gods?

I pondered this as I made my way back to the clearing, where Jasin had started a small fire in the center. Slade and Reven were tending to the horses, while Auric was studying the map. I got to work skinning the hare, but then Jasin took over cooking duties.

"I've got this covered," he said, with a cocky grin.

"Be my guest," I said, stepping back.

He pulled out some herbs from his packs and tended to the hare, then strung it up over the fire. I moved my bedroll farther away from the flames, then sank down onto it, remembering the last time I'd traveled like this. Back then I'd been alone and terrified, searching for somewhere safe to lay low for a while. At least now I had four men with me who seemed like they could handle themselves in combat, even without their new powers.

When the food was ready, the others settled in around the fire. I pulled out some of the cheese and fruit from Tash's mother, while Jasin sliced pieces of the hare and served it to us. The tempting aroma had all of us digging in immediately, and it didn't disappoint.

"This is really good," I told Jasin. "Where did you learn to cook?"

"From my mom, but also in the army. You pick up all sorts of skills there. I'm not bad with a sewing needle either. But food is my second love, so I made a point to learn to make some decent meals after choking down the other soldiers' terrible grub."

"What's your first love?" Slade asked.

Jasin smirked. "Women, of course."

"Of course." I rolled my eyes, while Slade chuckled and Auric shook his head. Reven just looked bored, which seemed to be normal for him.

Once we finished eating, I leaned back on my bedroll and stretched my aching limbs, feeling exhausted but not yet tired enough to go to sleep. "I'd like to get to know you all a little better. Maybe you can each tell me something about yourselves, like where you're from, or what your life was like before you met a God."

"Makes sense," Jasin said. "Guess we better get to know each other, since we're going to be bound together for the rest of our lives. Not just Kira, but all of us."

"Not me," Reven said, his voice cold.

"What do you mean?" Auric asked.

"I'm not going to be one of you."

Slade gave him a steely look. "We were selected for a purpose. The Water God chose you for a reason."

Reven broke a branch in half with a sharp *snap*. "Then he can choose another."

"Why are you even here then?" Jasin asked.

"I didn't have much of a choice," Reven said. "I couldn't deny the urge to reach Kira, same as all of you. But as soon as I find a way out of this mess, I'm gone. I have no desire to be a Dragon or to be anyone's mate."

Jasin's eyebrows drew together and he looked furious, and both Auric and Slade looked like they might respond, but I held up a hand.

"It's fine," I said. "None of us chose this. I understand if you don't want to be here. Gods know I don't want to be a part of this myself." I glanced between all of them, watching the fire's glow flicker on their masculine faces. "If there is a way out of this, you're all welcome to take it. I won't hold it against you. But at the moment we need to work together to get through this." I turned to Reven. "Can you do that?"

He gave me a cold look. "For now."

I supposed that was the best I'd get from him. "This isn't easy for me either. I never expected to suddenly have four men show up in my village and claim me as their mate, but here we are. Right now we're all strangers, but I'm hoping we can change that."

For some time, the only sound was the popping of the fire, but then Slade spoke up. "I'm from Clayridge, a town on the western side of the Earth Realm. Lived there my entire life working as a blacksmith, like my father. Not much more to tell really."

I was certain that wasn't true, but I didn't blame him for

not wanting to spill all his secrets to what were effectively a bunch of strangers he'd only met yesterday. At least he was trying.

"Ever been in a fight?" Jasin asked him.

"A few," Slade replied.

Jasin nodded, and everyone looked to him next. "My turn, I guess." He gestured at his uniform. "Pretty sure you've all guessed what I did before this. I come from a military family actually. Everyone in my family has served at one time or another. Grew up in the Fire Realm, but I've been all over as part of the Onyx Army."

"Are you still loyal to the Black Dragon?" Reven asked, his tone deceptively casual. I instantly tensed, worried the question might cause a problem, even if I'd been wondering the same thing. It was something no one would ever ask out loud, and something no one would ever deny. *Of course* we were all loyal to the Black Dragon. Everyone was, unless you wished to be cut down by her soldiers or her mates.

Jasin looked caught off guard, but then he stared into the flames with his jaw clenched. "I was, once. Not anymore."

I wanted to ask him what occurred to make his loyalties shift, but I wasn't sure now was the time. Was it being chosen by the Fire God? Or did something happen before that?

Auric cleared his throat. "Guess I'll go next. I'm from Stormhaven. I'm a...scholar, I guess you could say. I have a special interest in history, culture, geography, and religion. All of which might come in handy now, I hope."

Jasin snorted. "You're a nobleman. That much is obvious."

"Well, yes." Auric straightened up, raising his chin. "Is that a problem? If you doubt my usefulness in combat, I've been trained in sword fighting since I was a child."

"Ceremonial sword fighting, no doubt," Jasin muttered. "Maybe we should be asking *him* about his loyalties. All the noble families serve the Black Dragon too."

Auric narrowed his eyes at Jasin. "I'm loyal to this mission. Can the rest of you say the same?"

"That's enough," I said, feeling even more exhausted after listening to them bicker. It was a bad sign if they were fighting already. "No one is questioning anyone's loyalty." I turned toward Reven. "I assume you must be from the Water Realm then. What did you do before you were chosen?"

He leveled his dark gaze at me. "I killed people for money."

We all froze, staring at him as if to check that he was serious. Yes, he definitely was. An *assassin*. I supposed that explained all the black clothing and the way he'd killed Roark with silence and ease. But why would the Water God choose such a man for me?

Jasin forced a grin and broke the awkward silence. "Well, at least we know he'll be good in a fight."

15

JASIN

I coaxed a small flame to life on each of my fingertips. Even after a month with these powers, they never ceased to amaze me. I doubted having magic would ever get old. After all, who wouldn't want to be able to control fire?

The sun had only just breached the horizon, its light filtering through the thick trees around us. My companions were still asleep, but it was my turn on watch and I'd been passing the time playing with fire. Literally.

I'd moved to the other side of the stream, far enough from the camp that I wouldn't spook the horses or accidentally set fire to anything important, but close enough to keep an eye on my companions and watch for any threats. I summoned a ball of flame between my palms, making it hotter and hotter, until it burned blue underneath my fingers. I threw it as if it were a rock, aiming it at a cluster of large stones in the middle of the stream. The fiery ball flew across and hit the stones with a burst of embers and the hiss of steam.

A twig snapped behind me and I turned quickly, but it was only Kira. Her long red hair was messy from sleep and her eyes were huge, as if startled. I glanced around, but didn't see any signs of danger. Then I realized she was staring at the spot where I'd thrown the fire.

"Everything all right?" I asked.

She blinked and seemed to shake herself out of it. "Fine. Just half asleep."

I nodded, but I got the feeling there was more to it than that. Was she nervous about all of our powers? Or just mine?

"Should we wake the others?" I asked, glancing back at the other men. I wasn't sure what to think about any of them. Slade seemed like a decent enough guy, even if he didn't talk much. Auric was a useless nobleman who shouldn't even be on this journey. And Reven? I didn't trust him at all. I planned to keep my eye on him so none of us ended up with a knife in our backs.

Kira, on the other hand, was everything I could have hoped for. I'd never thought I could ever settle down with just one woman, but the second I'd met her, that worry had vanished. Sharing her with the other guys though... I wasn't sure I'd ever be okay with that. Sure, I'd shared women with other soldiers before for a night or two, but that was differ-ent. None of those women were mine. Not like Kira would be.

She moved beside me, leaning against the same thick

tree trunk that had been my backrest for the last hour. "We'll give them another few minutes to sleep. Were you practicing your magic?"

"I have to, since my new powers didn't come with any kind of training lesson or manual on how to use them. Good thing I seem to be immune to fire now, or I'd be dead many times over, or at least a whole lot crispier." I flashed her a grin. "The barracks I was living in? Not so lucky. But after a lot of practice over the last month, I'm learning to control what the Fire God's given me. Mostly."

She shivered and wrapped her arms around herself, even though it wasn't that cold. "Probably a good idea. Just be careful."

"Always," I said, conjuring another fireball over my open palm.

She flinched back, her eyes fixed on the flickering flame like it was a live snake. Maybe she wasn't scared of our magic—she was scared of fire. I closed my hand over the flame, dousing it immediately, and her shoulders relaxed.

"You don't need to be afraid," I said. "I'd never hurt you, Kira."

"I'm not afraid of you." She tore her gaze away and stared into the forest, then drew in a breath and faced me again. "Tell me about your encounter with the Fire God."

"It was pretty incredible. A giant made out of flames came to me in the middle of the forest and told me to find you. At first, I thought maybe I'd eaten one of those weird mushrooms in the forest again. Last time that happened I saw pink dancing water elementals for two days and had a raging headache for a week." I winked at her and she gave me a smile that made my heart beat faster. "But there was no denying this was all real and not a hallucination—not after I accidentally set my bed on fire."

"No wonder you're practicing," she said. "Is that when you left the Onyx Army?"

"Pretty much. Once I accepted that I really had been chosen by the Fire God I knew I had to quit. That turned out to be a lot harder than I expected. The Onyx Army wasn't exactly happy about one of their finest soldiers up and leaving for no real reason." *Not when he was so good at hunting the Resistance,* I mentally added. "But as the days went on, the tugging in my gut told me there was no other option. This was my destiny and I had to find you, no matter what. I escaped the army and became a deserter, even though it cost me everything. My job. My friends. Probably my family too."

"I'm sorry." She frowned as she glanced back at the camp. "It seems none of us want to be here on this journey."

"That's not true. Yes, I had to give up my previous life, but I do want to be here."

She sighed. "You might be the only one."

"Nah. We've all been ripped from our normal lives and given this larger-than-life destiny to fulfill with four strangers we're now stuck with, possibly forever. It's going to take some getting used to for all of us." I reached out and pushed back a stray piece of her red hair, smoothing it on her head. "But we'll get there, I promise."

"Thanks. I appreciate your confidence."

"Confidence is my specialty," I said, giving her an arrogant grin. She laughed, and the sound was so perfect I knew I'd do whatever it took to make her laugh like that again. How was it possible we'd only met yesterday?

"You're such a flirt," she said. "I bet you woo all the women you meet."

"I was quite popular with the ladies, it's true." I leaned against the tree and gazed into her eyes. "For good reason, I assure you."

She cocked her head. "Let me guess. You have a lover or two in every town you've visited, who are now all pining away, awaiting your return."

"Not quite. And every woman who shared my bed knew I wasn't making any promises."

An eyebrow darted up while her smile dropped. "Is that what I should expect as well?"

"No," I said quickly. "My past is behind me. From now on, I'm yours and yours alone. Assuming you want me as your mate, of course."

Our eyes locked and heat passed between us, but then she quickly looked away. "We should probably get ready."

She straightened, brushed herself off, and headed back to the main part of the camp. I watched her go, checking out her behind in those tight hunting leathers she wore, then sighed. I'd ruined the moment with my stupid mouth, and now she doubted my loyalty. Sure, I'd slept with lots of women, but that was before I'd met her. She couldn't hold that against me now.

I made another flaming ball, the frustration fueling my

magic and making it especially large, and then I hurled it at the stones with extra vigor. Unfortunately, I missed. The fire hit the grass on the other side of the stream, instantly setting it alight. Panic rose in my throat as the flames spread to a nearby tree, but I was too horrified to do anything. Gods, what had I done?

Water leaped up from the stream and covered the fire, dousing the flames with a loud sizzle. I turned and saw Reven standing in the shadow of the tree. He gave me a sharp look, before turning away. How long had he been there, spying on us?

Worst of all, Kira stood behind him. And she'd seen it all too.

16

KIRA

Once our camp was packed up, we continued traveling along the main road toward the Air Realm in the southeast. I rode with Reven first, needing some space from Jasin, especially after that last fireball. Thank the Gods Reven had put it out quickly before the flames took over the entire forest. How was I supposed to bond with Jasin when fear spiked through me every time he used his powers? Better yet, how was I supposed to face the Fire God? And after I did that, I'd be able to conjure fire myself—did I even want that?

Did I have a choice?

I tried to put the thoughts out of my head by focusing on the man sitting in front of me, but he wasn't exactly one for conversation. Our last exchange had gone like this:

"So, you're an assassin?" I'd asked Reven, after we'd been on the road for fifteen minutes.

"Yes," he'd said, his voice showing no emotion at all.

"How did you get involved in that kind of work?"

"It's a long story."

I'd waited for him to go on, but he seemed content to leave it at that. Giving up, I'd sighed and turned back to gazing at the forest and the mountains in the distance instead. Good thing the Water Temple was last, because I had a hard time seeing the two of us getting intimate anytime soon. Assuming Reven would even stick around that long.

We stopped for lunch in another clearing and then it was time for me to ride with Jasin, who still wore his military uniform. Even though I would never admit it out loud, it was a good look on him, complementing the red highlights in his hair and enhancing his broad shoulders. There was something about a man in uniform, and Jasin looked commanding, dangerous, and incredibly sexy.

"Don't you have something else you can wear?" I asked, as he helped me up onto his war horse. Unlike the others, he had me sit in front of him, and the solid presence of him behind me made my heart race.

He took the reins in front of me, his arms brushing against mine. "Not really. I only grabbed a few things when I left, and since I was traveling alone I figured it would be safer if I was in my uniform."

"Maybe, but it might draw attention now. It'll be hard to explain why you're traveling with the four of us. Plus a lot of people don't look fondly on the Onyx Army around here."

I felt him shrug. "It'll have to do for now. I can take the coat off when we enter a village."

"That could work, and once we get to a larger town we can see about getting you some other clothes."

He snorted. "Make sure to get some for Auric too then. He sticks out more than I do."

I cast a glance over at Auric, who sat straight on his white horse wearing clothes that looked more suitable for going to a ball than for traveling. "You have a point there."

We continued for another few hours through a bit of road that had thick trees on either side of it, cutting out a lot of the light. I nearly dozed off, with the horse moving rhythmically underneath me and Jasin's very warm body behind me. I almost leaned back and rested my head against him, but managed to restrain myself. My body was comfortable with him already, even if my mind wasn't yet.

As the hour grew late, we decided to stop at a village up ahead for the night so we could get supplies and feed the horses. But as we approached, it was immediately clear something was wrong.

We walked our horses slowly into the center of the village, their steps the only sound we could hear. The stone buildings around us had all been turned to little more than rubble, with huge pieces missing or crumbled to the ground. It seemed fairly recent, since the nearby forest hadn't taken over the ruins yet, but there was no sign of anyone still living here.

"What happened here?" Auric asked, as we spun around to take it all in.

"An elemental attack, most likely," Slade said, his tone grim. "The people must have abandoned the village afterward."

"I heard about a town that was attacked by rock elementals a month ago," I said, remembering the doomed travelers' words. "This could be the same place, or one that suffered a similar fate."

"If so, where are the elementals now?" Jasin asked, his hand on his sword as he glanced around.

"Perhaps the Dragons took care of them," Auric said, with a shrug.

"Unless the Jade Dragon is the one who did this," Slade said.

"It doesn't matter what happened," Reven said. "No one is here now. We should look around for any supplies they might have left behind and find a place to sleep for the night."

The thought of staying here in this abandoned town made my stomach twist. "What if the elementals return?"

He met my eyes. "Then we'll deal with them."

I still didn't like it, and the other men seemed wary as well, but they nodded and dismounted their horses. We did a quick search through the crumbled buildings, with Slade moving the stone so we could look for supplies or any sign of what had happened. We found very little, which made me think we weren't the first people to pick through these ruins.

We found a small building that was mostly intact except for one missing wall and decided to sleep there for the night. As I pushed aside the debris and laid out my things, I wondered what the building had once been used for before. A small house? A shop? It was hard to tell. I picked up a dusty old doll with only one leg and shuddered, before tossing it aside.

Between exhaustion and the eeriness of the place, none of us spoke much that night before we took to our beds. I fell asleep almost instantly, but it seemed as if only minutes had passed before Reven's voice woke me.

"Wake up," he said in a low voice. "We've got company."

I rose to a sitting position and blinked back sleep as his words settled over me. Reven had taken the first watch, and now he stood over the four of us with only the moonlight illuminating his dark frame. Outside, the night was silent. Maybe too silent.

Jasin jumped to his feet instantly. "What kind of company?"

"Not the friendly kind," Reven said.

"How many?" Slade asked.

Reven glanced through the missing wall, though I couldn't see anything out there. "Seven at least. Bandits, most likely. They're surrounding us now."

Jasin swore under his breath. "They must have been watching this town. Waiting for us to go to sleep so they could attack."

Yes, that was definitely their plan. I remembered as much from my short time living with a group of them myself.

"Can we get our horses and outrun them?" Auric asked, as he quickly pulled on his boots.

"Not likely," Reven said.

"Especially not with Kira sharing a horse," Jasin said. "But we could try."

"Run or fight?" Slade asked, turning his green eyes to me. The others waited for my answer too.

I swallowed. All my life I'd stayed in the shadows and kept to myself, trying to draw as little attention as possible. I wasn't used to being a leader and wasn't sure I liked this new role. What if I made the wrong decision and one of them was injured, or Gods forbid, worse? How could I live with that?

I went over everything they'd said. We were surrounded and couldn't outrun the bandits, not with me riding with one of them. We didn't know the land around here, and the bandits probably did. No matter what we chose we were at a disadvantage.

"Fight," I said, praying I'd made the right decision and wasn't leading my men to their deaths. I'd only known them for a few days, but I was already terrified of losing them.

"So be it," Jasin said, flashing a bloodthirsty smile. "I do love a good fight."

"We have to be careful not to use our powers though," Auric said. "We can't let anyone know who or what we are."

"Or we need to make sure no one is alive to speak a word about us," Reven said, pulling his hood over his head again.

With that grim thought, we quickly prepared ourselves and left the ruined building, since there was no room to fight inside it. As we stood in the center of the village, the men all drew their weapons and I gripped my bow tight. Jasin clutched his large sword, while Auric held a long, thin blade with elaborate carvings. Slade lifted his huge axe, his stance wide, like nothing was getting through him. Reven disappeared into the shadows or maybe onto a nearby roof, I wasn't sure.

Dark figures crept out of doorways and blades glinted under the starlight, but my rapid breathing was the only thing I could hear.

Auric raised his sword. "Here they come."

"Protect Kira," Slade told the others.

Jasin gripped his weapon tighter. "With my life."

"I can protect myself," I told them, readying my bow. I prayed to the Gods it was true.

17

KIRA

As dark figures approached from all around us I nocked an arrow, my heart pounding in my chest. We were outnumbered and would soon be surrounded. What if I'd made the wrong decision?

When the first bandit came within range, I released my arrow. It struck the man in the chest and he hit the ground. I grabbed another arrow immediately, but by then the attackers were already upon us.

Thin knives appeared from the rooftops above us, landing in the throats of two of the bandits, killing them instantly. Thrown by Reven, no doubt. He leaped off the rooftop and his twin blades sliced through another bandit as he landed. He then launched himself at the next attacker in a blur of movement.

Slade swung his axe at a man wearing a gray hood, while

Auric's long blade clashed with a curved sword wielded by a woman. Jasin moved in front of me, meeting two bandits with his heavy sword, his movements swift and powerful. He spun and slashed between the two of them, keeping them at bay.

Everything happened so quickly it was hard to tell who was friend or foe in the darkness, and I hesitated to release my arrow while wishing I could be of more help in the fight. When Auric narrowly dodged a blow from the woman with the curved sword, I saw my chance and let my arrow fly, taking her down with a well-placed shot in the chest.

The two men fighting Jasin pushed him back against a wall and I saw a burst of blood under the moonlight. Panic shot through me and I readied another arrow to help defend him, but then a woman lunged at me with a dagger. Auric let out a shout and blasted a gust of wind toward her, sweeping her off her feet—and me along with her.

I hit the ground hard on my back, all the air knocked from my chest and my head smarting from the impact. The bandit woman recovered faster and grabbed her dagger off the ground, already getting back to her feet. I sucked in a breath and lifted myself up, but I wasn't quick enough in reaching for my own knife from my boot. She raised her dagger, but then a barrage of rubble slammed into her, courtesy of Slade I assumed.

Only problem was the rocks went wide and smashed into Jasin and Auric too. Flames lashed out from Jasin's hands at the two bandits in front of him, setting them both on fire, along with everything around them. In an instant, the nearby brush was alight and blazing with heat.

Behind me, Reven swore under his breath and conjured a downpour of water over the flames like he'd done this morning, except on a larger scale. A *much* larger scale. Suddenly we were up to our knees in a flash flood of muddy water, which swept two of the bandits away into the forest. I grabbed onto a nearby piece of rubble to steady myself as the water rushed around me.

Within seconds, all our attackers were either dead or gone. I wasn't sure if any of them had escaped or not. If they did, then our secret would be out.

A body floated up beside me and I shuddered, while our nearby horses stomped their feet in the rising water. I lifted my bow above the water and each of my men looked somewhere between stunned and exhausted, which was about how I felt too. We were all soaked through, covered in mud and blood with a few cuts and bruises, but at least we were alive.

"Is everyone all right?" I asked.

Jasin touched his neck, which was still bleeding. "Nothing serious."

"I'm fine," Auric said.

Reven regarded the ruined village like he still expected trouble to emerge from its dark doorways. "We should get moving."

"No kidding," Jasin said, as he trudged through the knee-high muddy stream. "Think you summoned enough water here?"

Reven's eyes narrowed at him. "I wouldn't have had to use my powers at all if you hadn't set the entire place on fire."

"That wouldn't have happened if Slade hadn't attacked me with a pile of rocks," Jasin snapped.

"That was an accident," Slade said.

"We all made mistakes," Auric said, glancing at me. "I'm sorry I hit you also."

"We're still alive," I said. "That's what matters. We just have some things to work on, that's all."

"That's an understatement," Jasin muttered.

We made it to the horses and began packing up quickly, all of us eager to get away from this wretched place. But then Slade stopped just before mounting his horse and moved to rest his hand against a large rock nearby. All of us paused to watch him, wondering what he was doing. He closed his eyes and stood there, his palm pressing on the smooth stone, before finally pulling away. "There's a cave nearby. We can camp there tonight."

"Now you tell us," Jasin said, throwing up his hands.

"I didn't feel its presence before." Slade frowned. "Actually, I didn't know I could do that until now."

"Fascinating." Auric said. "I suspect we'll all discover new uses of our powers the more we use them."

Reven mounted his horse in one quick movement. "Let's go."

As Jasin pulled me up onto the horse behind him, he flinched a little. His neck was soaked in blood from the wound he'd received earlier. The wound he'd gotten defending me.

I lightly touched his neck, inspecting the gash. "We should take care of this."

"I'm fine," Jasin said, as he flicked the reins of his horse. "Just a scratch."

"We should at least clean it and wrap it." As we left the abandoned village behind us, I covered his wound with my hand, trying to stop the flow of blood. It was the only thing I could do while we were riding. Warmth flared as we touched, making my fingertips tingle against his skin.

"It's not so bad, really. I've had worse while shaving." Despite his words, he rested his hand over mine, like he didn't want me to pull it away. I became acutely aware of how close we were, with my fingers on his neck and my other hand on his hip. But I didn't pull away either.

I ran my thumb slowly along his skin. "I just hate seeing any of you hurt."

"Ah, so you do care about me."

"You may be growing on me a little," I admitted.

"I knew it." He flashed me a roguish grin over his shoulder.

"Don't get—" I started, but then I pulled my hand away to check the flow of blood and the rest of the words caught in my mouth. Jasin's neck was not only no longer bleeding, but it didn't seem to be injured at all anymore. How...?

"What is it?" Jasin asked, twisting on the saddle to look back at me. Auric glanced over at us, his brow furrowed, while Slade stopped his horse.

"Your neck," I said, running my fingers over it, not believing my eyes. "The wound. It's gone."

Jasin touched the area where he'd been cut with a frown. "Gods, you're right."

"Kira must have healed it," Auric said.

"Me?" I asked. "I didn't do anything."

Slade shrugged. "You're the representative of the Spirit Goddess and the next Black Dragon. It makes sense you would have some powers of your own."

Jasin stretched his neck, but he didn't seem to be in any pain anymore. "Incredible."

Auric examined Jasin closely. "I've heard rumors that the Black Dragon can heal her mates. I should have realized that would apply to us as well."

I stared down at my hand, which was still coated in Jasin's blood. "When I touched Jasin my hand felt warm, but he's always warm so I didn't think much of it. Maybe that's how I did it?"

"Is anyone else injured?" Auric asked.

Slade shook his head, and we turned to Reven, who'd been watching the entire conversation in silence. When all eyes fell upon the small cut on his forehead, he sighed. "Fine, you can heal me."

I slid off of Jasin's horse and climbed up behind Reven. I was even more hesitant to touch him than Jasin, but I braced myself and lightly rested my hand over Reven's forehead. While Jasin was comforting and warm, like sitting near a hearth on a cold night, Reven was cool and soothing, like diving into a refreshing lake on a hot day. That same tingling feeling returned to my fingertips, and when I pulled my hand away, the cut on his forehead had vanished.

"Praise the Gods," Slade said quietly.

I stared at my hand. Even though I hadn't been given any direction by the Spirit Goddess, it seemed she'd given me a gift too. Praise the Gods indeed.

KIRA

As the moon climbed the sky, Slade guided our horses through the forest toward the mountains and the cave he'd sensed. The entrance to it was so small that none of us could squeeze inside, but he used his powers to push some of the stones away so we could enter.

We spread out around the cave and Jasin started a fire, while Auric created a breeze so the smoke would travel outside. Slade made a circle of stone, which Reven filled up with water, allowing us to wash ourselves and our clothes as best we could to get the mud and blood off. I took care of the horses, rubbing them down and giving them a few slices from an apple. They all butted their heads against my hand, wanting my attention. No surprise, really. Animals had always liked me. A coincidence, or because I was the representative of the Spirit Goddess? I wasn't sure.

After washing our clothes, we hung them on rocks near

the fire so they would dry by morning. I'd donned one of my fraying dresses, while Jasin had opted to go shirtless, wearing only trousers after claiming he was hot. I tried not to stare at his naked chest and failed horribly. Who could blame me, with all those muscles on display and that intriguing trail of dark hair going down into his pants? He smirked at me, like he knew I was enjoying the show, and I swallowed and forced myself to look away.

None of us were ready to sleep yet after a fight like that, even though we were all exhausted. Instead we spread out around the fire and ate some of the dried meat, bread, and fruit we had stored in our packs.

"Let's admit it," Jasin said, as he leaned back on his bedroll in a way that flaunted his well-developed chest. "Tonight was a disaster. We got lucky, but it could have gone another way easily."

Auric smoothed back his blond hair, which looked darker since it was still wet. "We simply need more training. Not just on our own, but as a team."

"You should practice fighting against each other too," I said. "And then once you're all masters, you can teach me. Since supposedly I'll be inheriting these powers soon." I couldn't decide if I was excited about the idea or nervous. The guys could barely control their powers with just one element and I was supposed to master all four somehow. Including fire. I shuddered just thinking about it. But until I got those powers, I'd be at a disadvantage too. I was pretty good with my bow, but my fighting skills were a bit rusty otherwise.

"At least you can patch us up when we get injured," Slade said.

"Hopefully that won't happen too often, but I suppose I need to practice that also. Or even just figure out how I did it." I sighed and wiped bread crumbs off my lap. "You each fought well earlier. Maybe you could teach me some tricks too."

"I'd be happy to teach you lots of things," Jasin said, with a naughty grin that made me shake my head, even though I was secretly a little bit tempted.

"Training with each other is a good way to pass the time while we're in camp," Auric said. "We have many nights ahead of us while we travel to the different temples."

"I have something we can use to pass the time tonight." Slade reached inside his bag, then pulled out a large dark bottle.

"What's that?" I asked.

"Whiskey. Finest in the Earth Realm." He chuckled softly. "Okay, that's not true, but it was cheap at least."

Slade poured us each a bit of whiskey and we all relaxed as we took a sip. After a few minutes, even Reven looked less tense than usual. With the alcohol warming me from the inside out, I felt more comfortable around the guys than I had before. Even though things had gone wrong tonight, we'd fought together, bled together, and all had each other's backs. That kind of experience created a bond like nothing else could. Or maybe that was just the alcohol talking.

As Slade poured me a refill, he said, "Last night you

asked us about where we're from and what we did before this. I think it's time you told us more about yourself, Kira."

My fingers tightened around my cup. "What do you want to know?"

"Everything," Auric said with a warm smile. "Did you always live in Stoneham?"

My past was not something I liked to talk about. Even Tash knew very little about my life before I showed up in her inn looking for a job. But these men were supposed to be my mates. I had to tell them something, and maybe someday I'd feel comfortable enough to tell them more. "No, I only lived there for the last three years or so. Before that I traveled around a lot."

"Where were you from originally?" Slade asked, as his fingers ran through his dark beard in a very distracting way. "Somewhere else in the Earth Realm?"

"I grew up in the Water Realm, actually. A small town on the coast called Tidefirth." Thinking back to those happy years made my throat tighten with emotion. "But I've lived in all of the Realms at some point or another, for a short while at least."

"Sounds like you were on the run from something. Or someone." Reven gazed at me from under his dark hood with those brooding blue eyes that seemed to peer deep into my soul.

I looked into Jasin's eager brown eyes next, then Auric's intelligent gray ones, and Slade's calm green ones. Each man stared at me, but none of them pressured me to reveal more about my past. But I would have to take a leap at some point. Might as well be now.

I drew in a breath. "My family was killed by the Crimson Dragon when I was thirteen." My hands wrung together in my lap, while I forced the next words out. "He burned down our entire house with my parents still in it. The memory has haunted me for my entire life."

Jasin reached over and grabbed my hand. "I'm so sorry."

"That must have been horrible," Slade said.

"It was." I shuddered as I remembered the flames, the smoke, the screams, and worst of all, the smell. "I only survived because my parents made me hide, after warning me that the Dragons would kill me if they ever found me. I didn't realize it at the time, but I think they were part of the Resistance. They knew the Dragons would come for me too because of that. I've been laying low ever since."

Auric took my other hand and gave it a squeeze. "Could your parents have known what you are?"

"I doubt it," I said. "How could they have known? Even I didn't know until the four of you showed up. Did any of you think something like this would happen?"

"Not a chance," Reven muttered.

Slade shook his head. "I still barely believe it."

"What did you do after your parents were killed?" Auric asked.

"I was so terrified that I fled my home as soon as I could. Hitched a ride with some traveling merchants at first. I moved around a lot after that until I landed in Stoneham." There was more, of course, but I'd already mentioned my parents' deaths. I didn't need to drag up any other bad memories tonight.

Before they could ask me any more questions, I downed the rest of my whiskey. "I'm exhausted. I think I'll hit the sack."

"Need some company?" Jasin asked, sitting up and drawing my eyes back to his naked and very appealing chest.

"Not a chance," I managed to say.

He shrugged, with a sinful smile on his lips. "The offer is always open in case you'd like to practice before we arrive at the Fire Temple."

I ignored him as I prepared for bed, although I wondered if practicing wasn't a bad idea. But the other three men were all watching us, and I knew they'd heard what he'd offered. Would they be jealous when Jasin was the first to bond with me? Or grateful it didn't have to be one of them?

19

REVEN

With my arms crossed, I kept a wary eye on Jasin as he threw streams of fire toward the wall of the cave. I'd already had to put out his flames twice yesterday. I wouldn't be surprised if I had to do it again now. The man was reckless and out of control, although I had to admit he was a skilled fighter. I wouldn't want to face him in combat, but I didn't trust him not to get us all killed either.

Outside the cave, Slade lifted small pebbles and tossed them at Auric, who blasted them away with a strong gust. A blacksmith and a nobleman. I had little in common with either one and no desire to know them better. I got the feeling they were both hiding something too, but then again, who among us wasn't?

On the other side of the cave, Kira was packing up the last of our camp so we could get back on the road soon. I caught myself staring at her as she straightened up and threw her bag over her shoulder, admiring the curves of her body in that thin dress and the way her hair brushed against her graceful neck. I turned away with a frown. I shouldn't be looking at her like that. Not when I had no plans to make her mine.

"Are you going to practice your magic too?" she asked, as she walked over to me.

"I'm fine." I didn't plan on keeping these powers much longer either.

She tilted her head and examined me. "I suppose you don't need magic to stay safe anyway. Where did you learn to fight like that?"

I gave her the side-eye. Once again, she was trying to learn about my past. If only she knew how similar our childhoods had been. But I never talked about that. "Here and there."

She sighed and began to turn away. "I get it. You don't want to talk to me."

Something ached in my chest at the disappointment in her voice. No doubt because of this stupid magical connection between us, nothing more. It made me desire her and care for her, even if I didn't want to. Gods, I couldn't wait for this spell to be broken.

"My father taught me," I reluctantly said. "He was a great swordsman."

She paused and considered me again. "Do you think you could teach me as well? I'd like to be able to fight better at close range."

"I can do that." If we were training, I wouldn't have to

talk about my past or think about how much I wanted her. I drew both of my swords and handed one of them to her.

She examined the finely crafted blade, which was black and carved with elaborate designs. "This is beautiful. Your father's?"

"They were, yes." I gripped the matching blade in my hand. "How much do you know about sword fighting?"

"I've been trained in the basics before and I'm pretty good with a dagger." She got into position, holding the blade out as if ready for an attack. "Maybe you can give me some tips and help me practice."

"First of all, you'd be better off holding the sword like this." I moved close and adjusted her fingers on the hilt. As we touched, the connection between us snapped into place, like when she'd healed me yesterday. I jerked my hand away and stepped back quickly. "See if that's better."

She swung the sword and nodded. "I think so."

"Let's see what we're working with." I lunged toward her, moving slower than I normally did. She raised her blade to meet mine with some hesitation, her movements a bit jerky. I swung again and she managed to dodge, then sliced toward me. I parried her, but with each second, I could tell her confidence was growing as she remembered how to use a sword. She'd clearly had some training before, but she was out of practice and still had a lot to learn.

"Not bad," I said. "Where did you learn to fight?"

"The merchants taught me a little, and the rest..." Her face paled and she looked away. "I'd rather not say right now. We all have things in our past we'd prefer not to discuss."

"That we do." I gestured for her to attack me again.

We did another round, and by the end of it she was breathing quickly, her chest rising and falling in a way that made it hard not to stare at her full breasts. I couldn't deny she was beautiful, or that I wanted her in my bed. That would be true even without the damn magic tugging me toward her. It simply made it harder to resist her. But I'd lived my entire life exercising control over myself and my surroundings, and I wasn't about to let a pretty face and alluring body ruin all of that.

As I stared at her, she managed to catch me off guard and almost landed a blow. "Aha!" she said, laughing.

I scowled at her. "I let you get that one to boost your confidence."

"Of course you did," she teased.

We were about to go again, when Auric suddenly let out a pained sound, and we both turned toward him. Kira rushed out of the cave, with me right at her heels and Jasin a step behind us. I was instantly alert, worried the bandits had returned. Or worse, that the elementals had found us.

Auric was on the ground, nursing a cut on his cheek. "It's nothing. Slade nicked me with a rock."

Slade offered Auric his hand to help him up. "Sorry about that."

"It was my fault, I missed that one," Auric said, as he stood up and brushed himself off.

Kira moved close to Auric, inspecting his face. "I suppose it gives me a good excuse to practice healing you."

She brushed her fingers against the gash on his cheek, while he stared at her with lovesick eyes. Pathetic. Except as she caressed his face, jealousy boiled up in me. I wanted her to touch me like that, not him. Gods, now I was the pathetic one.

She pulled back and smiled at Auric. "All fixed."

"My thanks." He took her hand and pressed a kiss to it. "You're truly amazing, Kira."

Jasin grinned at her. "Now we're going to get injured just so you have an excuse to touch us."

She shook her head with an amused smile. "Please don't."

A strange sound came from the east, overhead. A huge gust of wind. The flap of large wings. The rustle of many trees.

I knew that sound.

"Get in the cave!" I grabbed Kira's arm and dragged her inside before she could protest. "Hurry!"

"What is it?" Slade asked, as the others rushed inside behind us.

"A Dragon," I said.

"What?" Kira's eyes went wide, but she didn't pull away from me, and I didn't release her arm. I didn't trust these other guys to protect her the way I could. None of them knew the danger that was coming for us, not the way I did. Kira knew, though. She understood all too well what the Dragons could do.

"Quick, cover the mouth of the cave," Auric told Slade.

Slade gestured and some of the large rocks moved in front of the cave entrance, though they left a small enough opening for us to peer through. We each crowded around it and watched as the dragon appeared over the forest, his large wings spread wide, casting huge shadows on the trees. Dark blue scales flashed under the sun, and even from this distance his sharp talons were visible, as was his long tail.

The Azure Dragon circled overhead twice, as if looking for something, before finally moving on. The cave was entirely silent while we watched him, as if we were each holding our breath, and only when he disappeared from sight did we all take a collective exhale.

"Was he looking for us?" Kira asked, her voice barely above a whisper.

"No way," Jasin said. "How would he know about us?"

Auric frowned as he gazed at the sky. "Some of the bandits might have gotten away and started spreading rumors about people with magic. Maybe he heard them somehow."

"Or maybe it was a coincidence and he's looking for someone else," Slade said.

I realized I was still holding Kira close even though the danger had passed. I quickly released her. "It doesn't matter. We need to get moving anyway."

I glanced back at the sky, at the spot where the Azure Dragon had soared over us. That was supposed to be me one day.

Not if I could help it.

20

KIRA

We stayed off the road as much as we could, eager to remain out of sight between the bandit attack and the Azure Dragon flying over us. I mentally shuddered remembering his dark wings soaring through the sky and that long tail stretched behind him.

I'd seen him once before when I was fourteen. He'd come to a village in the Air Realm I'd been visiting with the traveling merchants. I'd wandered off to pet some kittens in the inn's stables when the Azure Dragon, Doran, swooped down and landed in the center of the town. I'd peered through the wooden slats of the stables as he changed back into a tall man with blond hair that hung past his shoulders. I was terrified he was going to flood the entire village or drown someone, but all he did was talk to one of the merchants briefly before casting his gaze in the direction of the stables. His eyes were cold and piercing, and I had the horrible sense that he would find me and finish the job the Crimson Dragon had started. But then he turned away, shifted back into his dragon form, and flew off without a word.

Just to be safe, I'd left the village that night on my own. The merchant family had treated me well, almost like another daughter, and I hated abandoning them without a word, but the memory of my parents' deaths convinced me they would be safer without me around. Later I decided I'd been paranoid, that it was a mere coincidence that the Azure Dragon had shown up while we were there. He had no reason to look for me.

Now I wasn't so sure.

None of us seemed to feel like chatting much throughout the day, and we made good progress toward the Air Realm without encountering any danger. When night began to fall we paused near a larger town, and Auric pulled out his map.

"We should stop there for the evening," he said. "According to this map it's a town called Rockworth and should be large enough for us to buy some new clothes."

Reven frowned. "It would be safer if we avoided towns entirely."

"The horses need to eat and rest," Jasin said. "And so do we."

Slade rubbed his dark beard. "We should stock up on supplies too if we're going to be avoiding towns in the future. Especially since we didn't get anything from that village yesterday."

I gazed at the wooden roofs of the town, barely visible over the stone wall surrounding it with a small moat, likely to protect it from elementals. "Let's stop for the night, but be especially cautious while we're there. Auric, maybe you can borrow clothes from Reven or Slade so you don't stand out as much."

The men grumbled, but we stopped in the forest so they could change their clothes. I was already wearing one of my ragged dresses with my cloak over it. Jasin kept his black trousers from his uniform but donned a plain gray shirt from his pack. Auric's fine silk clothes went in his bag, and Slade gave him a pair of brown trousers, while Reven reluctantly let Auric use one of his black shirts. They didn't fit Auric perfectly, but they were good enough for now.

Once we all looked like any other group of weary travelers, we headed for the town. I rode with Auric, breathing in his clean, fresh scent as I held onto his back. Of all the men, I felt the most comfortable with him so far, which surprised me. On the surface we had little in common, but something about his cool, logical mind put me at ease. I also appreciated that he wanted to learn as much about me as he could, and the way he flattered me with his attention. And unlike Jasin, he seemed to want me for more than just sex.

Auric's horse led us to the open gates, where the Onyx Army had guards posted to inspect everyone who went in or out. They regarded us suspiciously and I grew nervous they'd stop us. Reven slipped some coins into their palms as if he'd done it a hundred times before, and then they let us go through with barely a second glance.

Rockworth was more than double the size of Stoneham and many other horses and carriages filled the road, along with people walking along the side of it. We passed a bustling market with men and women selling their wares, before stopping at the first inn we saw.

The inn was called the Knight's Reprieve and was crowded with dozens of travelers in the tavern grabbing some supper. Slade and Auric arranged for us to get the last two rooms, before we headed into the tavern ourselves. The room smelled faintly of warm food and was loud with the sounds of eating, talking, and music from a man playing fiddle in the corner. Reven slipped through the crowd easily and managed to grab us the last free table, but it only had four chairs.

"It's fine," Slade said. "I'll sit at the bar and see if I can get any information from the other travelers."

"Good idea," Auric said.

As Slade took a stool at the bar, Jasin pulled out a chair at the table for me, before immediately claiming the one to my right. Auric got a journal out of his bag and began jotting down some notes, while Reven sat against the wall, his arms crossed as he eyed everyone in the tavern with suspicion.

A waitress with a low-cut dress that probably got her a lot of tips came over to our table, and her face lit up when she saw the man at my side. "Jasin! What are you doing here?"

Jasin flashed her the same charming grin he often gave me. "Just stopping in for a night."

"Is that so?" She leaned close, accentuating her ample cleavage. "I'm so happy you're back in town."

"It's good to see you, Minda. How've you been?"

"Good, but even better now that you're here," she said, batting her eyelashes. "My sister will be excited to know you're back too."

"Tell her I said hello," he replied, while my fists clenched under the table. That familiar possessiveness rose up in me again, and this time it was harder to push down. Jasin and the others were supposed to be my mates and all, but even ignoring that, I'd spent the last few days traveling with them, sleeping near them, and fighting alongside them. Maybe I had a little bit of a right to be possessive at this point.

"I will." She trailed a hand lightly along his shoulders and her voice turned sultry. "And if you need a room tonight, ours is free."

He cleared his throat, glancing at me. "Thanks for the offer, but I've got a room."

"Too bad. We had a lot of fun last time. Let me know if you change your mind." She removed her hand, casting me a quick, appraising look. "I'll get you all some food."

After she walked away, I turned to Jasin, my blood boiling. "You slept with *both* sisters?"

"I did, yeah." His eyebrows darted up. "Long before I met you. Is that a problem?" He gestured at the other men. "And should you really judge me when you're going to sleep with all four of us?"

"I'm not judging, I'm just—" The words died on my

mouth and I looked away, still seething.

"What? Jealous?"

"No!" My cheeks flushed, because that's exactly how I was feeling.

He gave me that infuriatingly sexy grin. "I told you my bed's always open to you."

"Me and every other woman, it seems." I jumped to my feet, making the guys glance up at me with worried expressions. "I just need a moment. Feel free to start eating without me."

I headed out the front door of the inn, then walked around the side of it until I was near the stables and away from everyone else. My heart raced, and I felt like I couldn't breathe. Gods, why was I so upset? I'd only met Jasin a few days ago and we'd never made any promises to each other. What he did in the past—or even now—wasn't any of my business. He'd already admitted that he liked women. Lots of women. Which was fine, really. I didn't have any real claim over him, just some weird magical bond drawing us together. Without that, we would be strangers. So why did it hurt so badly when I saw him flirting with that woman?

"Kira, are you okay?" Auric asked.

I turned toward him, trying to keep my face blank. "I'm fine. Just needed some fresh air."

He moved closer, making me keenly aware of his height. "This situation is strange and overwhelming for all of us, but especially for you, I'm sure. It makes sense you would need to take a break from it now and then. But I just want you to know I'm here if you ever need to talk about it."

"Thank you. I appreciate that." I ran a hand through my hair and sighed. "I'm not sure it's possible to take a break from it either. This is my life now, and for better or worse, I'm stuck with the four of you. And you're all stuck with me."

Auric touched my cheek, his stormy eyes locked on mine. "I don't know about the other guys, but I'm glad I'm stuck with you."

"You are?" I asked, resting my hand over his. I remembered the moment we'd shared this morning when I'd healed him, and my eyes dropped to his mouth. I'd wanted to kiss him then, but the other guys had been watching. Now we were alone.

"I know you think none of us want to be here, but I do. Everything about this feels right." He lowered his head, his fingers tracing my lips. "Including this."

With one hand on my jaw he pressed his mouth to mine, while his other hand slid to my lower back to pull me against him. Sparks flashed between us as he teased my lips open, before stroking me slowly with his tongue. With a soft gasp, I wrapped my arms around his neck, wanting even more. It had been way too long since anyone had kissed me, but my body seemed to remember how to respond. Or maybe it was Auric who did that to me.

At first, I'd thought Auric might be snobbish or distant with his fine clothes and his head always buried in a book, but his kiss was anything but. He took his time with my mouth, learning what I responded to most, and soon he made me forget everything I'd been upset about. All I could think about was this rush of desire that swept through me at his touch, and how I wanted more.

"What the..." Jasin's voice said from behind me, interrupting the moment.

Auric and I broke apart, although he kept his hand on my back as we turned to face Jasin. My soldier looked stunned and maybe a little angry, but he was still mouth-wateringly handsome. That would never change, I supposed. And with lust already coursing through me thanks to Auric's kiss, it was hard not to want Jasin too. An image flashed in my head of being pressed between them with both their hands and mouths on me that sent heat straight to my core.

"Jasin." I wasn't sure what else to say. I didn't know if I should feel guilty for kissing Auric or not. Soon I'd be kissing all of them, if everything went according to plan, but I still had no idea how to handle this or how to juggle the feelings of four men. Or my overwhelming attraction to each of them.

"Could we have a moment alone?" Jasin asked Auric.

Auric glanced at me. "Are you all right with that?"

I nodded. "Yes, I'm fine. Thank you for making sure I was okay."

"Any time." He brushed his lips across mine, then straightened and gave Jasin a smug look before heading into the inn. I could practically feel the tension crackling in the air between them, and this new development would only make it worse.

Jasin swallowed, and my eyes couldn't help but linger on his strong neck dusted with stubble. "You kissed him."

"What? Jealous?" I asked, throwing his earlier words back at him.

"I am, yeah." He looked down at the ground, with a strand of hair falling over his forehead that I itched to brush away. "I thought I would be the first."

My heart softened at the vulnerability in his voice. "You're going to be the first in other things."

"I know. And I'm sorry about what happened in there. I swear, all of that is in the past. Nothing is going to happen with Minda or her sister or any other woman." His words warmed my chest, but then he blew out a breath. "But seriously, *that* guy?"

And now my heart hardened again. "What's your problem with Auric?"

"He's a stuffy nobleman!" Jasin's eyes flared, his jaw clenching. "Although maybe you like that sort of thing. He is rich, after all."

I propped my hands on my hips. "I like him because he's smart and kind and attentive, not because of his money. I don't care about any of that. And if you want to stay in this group, you're going to have to find a way to get along with him too."

I brushed past him as I made my way into the inn, my whole body flushed with both desire and anger. I'd never understand how Jasin could be so damn sexy while driving me crazy at the same time. And I was supposed to bond with him in only a few days? Not likely.

21

SLADE

I sat on the windowsill and observed the empty town lit with only moonlight and a few torches. I'd been on guard duty for an hour, but everything had been quiet so far. Nevertheless, I would remain vigilant to protect Kira and her other mates from any possible threats for the next few hours, when Auric would take my place.

Kira rose from the bed beside me and silently headed into the washroom. Jasin slept in the other bed, face down and completely out. He was a true soldier, able to fall into sleep the second his head touched the pillow and instantly alert the moment he got up. I had no doubt if I woke him now he'd be ready to fight on a second's notice. The boy was a hothead, but I never once doubted his loyalty to Kira or his willingness to do whatever it took to keep her safe.

The other two, I wasn't so sure. Auric seemed a decent fellow, but I was wary of him due to his background. I didn't have any great love for noblemen, but he was smart, I'd give him that. He seemed to be interested in Kira as well, but was it for the right reasons? Or did he only want to be a part of this for the knowledge and power he could uncover along the way?

And Reven? I didn't trust him at all, but he could have walked away a hundred times already, and he hadn't. I planned to keep an eye on him, but I didn't think he would put Kira in danger, not after how he'd defended her from the bandits. Even though he was distant now, I had a feeling he would come around eventually. If not, I'd be happy to show him the door. We had no room on this team for people who weren't committed to our mission.

As I watched through the window, something caught my eye outside the stone fence. An air elemental. It glided along the perimeter of the town and looked like a swirling tornado with arms and glowing eyes. I'd seen a few elementals before, mostly rock and water ones, but never an air type.

Elementals were immune to their own element, so Auric would be useless against this one, but they were weak against the others. The Dragons were supposed to keep us safe from them, but elemental attacks were common enough that people had learned how to defend themselves from them. Of course, that hadn't helped the village we'd visited last night. They'd clearly been unprepared for whatever had hit them and had fled the village instead of fighting back. But larger towns like this one were well fortified against elemental attacks. Other than the stone wall and the small moat, they also had a line of kindling next to a brazier they could easily light. I had no doubt that the guards were all trained in how to handle elementals as well, but I kept watch on the one below anyway.

We were just lucky it wasn't a shade. They were even more rare than elementals, but deadlier—and very little could stop them.

When Kira returned from the washroom, she spotted me and paused. She wore her one chemise, which was thin enough to show off her curves and the outline of her pale breasts, though I forced myself not to stare. If I looked at her like that I might start feeling things I had no desire to feel.

"Can't sleep?" I asked, my voice low so it wouldn't wake Jasin.

She shook her head as she sat beside me on the windowsill. "How's guard duty?"

"Quiet so far, although now we have a visitor." I pointed at the air elemental as it hovered outside the wall.

Her eyes widened as she caught sight of it. "Should we be worried?"

"Not yet. It seems to be alone, and it can't get through the town's wall. If it did, the guards could probably handle it. But I'm keeping an eye on it in case I need to help fight it off."

She nodded. "Let's hope it's just the one."

I leaned back and let my gaze linger on her a little longer. Her long red hair hung about her shoulders and a frown touched her lush lips. She'd worn that frown ever since she'd run out of the inn earlier tonight. I had a feeling Auric and Jasin were involved, judging by their similar expressions, but I wasn't sure if it was any of my business. Still, I didn't like seeing her upset.

"You seem troubled," I said.

"Is it that obvious?" She sighed. "Auric kissed me, Jasin's an ass, and Reven won't talk to me. You're the only one I can stand to be around at the moment."

"I'm honored," I said, with a low chuckle.

She took a piece of her hair and began idly twirling it as she looked out the window. "I don't know how to do this. I wasn't prepared to be involved with one man right now, let alone four."

I couldn't stop staring at her. She was too damn beautiful, and she made my resolve to keep my distance from her crumble. "You'll figure it out."

"I have to, I suppose." Her bright eyes found mine again in the darkness. "Do you ever wonder why we were chosen and not someone else?"

"Every damn day," I muttered.

"Me too. I can't stop questioning it all. Was I chosen for all of you, or were you chosen for me? What if the Gods chose wrong?"

"I've considered that too, but we must trust that they have a plan for us."

Her lips quirked up slightly. "Your faith in them is inspiring."

I shrugged. "I need to believe, otherwise I question everything too. Especially my place in this. I'm a simple blacksmith, nothing more. I don't belong here."

"Do you want to leave?" she asked softly.

"No. Not at all." I shook my head. "I'm sorry if I made it sound that way. I'm loyal to you and to our mission. Have no doubt about that."

"But you don't really want to be here."

"It's not that." I ran a hand along my beard as I considered my words. "It's more that I had a life I was content with already. A life I had no desire to leave behind."

"I see." She said, her voice quiet. "Did you leave someone behind?"

My chest clenched and at first, I couldn't respond. "No," I finally said. "There was someone once, but it's over."

Outside the window, the air elemental began moving toward the hills, leaving the town alone. My shoulders relaxed as he drifted out of sight. I didn't want to fight anyone unless it was absolutely necessary, even an elemental.

"It's gone," I said, turning back to Kira. "And you should head back to bed."

"I don't know if I can sleep."

Before I could stop myself, I said, "I can help. Turn around."

She shifted on the windowsill so that her back was to me. I took hold of her luxurious red hair and considered wrapping it around my hand and pulling her head back so I could claim her mouth, but I restrained myself and simply moved it over her shoulder. Over the chemise, I rested my hands on her upper back, immediately feeling the tension in it. Her upper body was strong, probably from her skill with a bow, and I smoothed my hands across her, slowly kneading her muscles. She tipped back her head with a breathy sigh that made me instantly hard.

"That's it, relax," I said, my breath close to her ear.

"I'm the one who is supposed to be healing you," she said.

"This is a different kind of healing." My hands moved up to her shoulders and she let out a soft groan as I worked the muscles there. I hadn't touched a woman like this in so long, and I hated to admit that I was enjoying it as much as she was. Compared to my large size she was so small and feminine, with soft skin and an inner strength that made her even more irresistible.

She relaxed against me and I trailed my fingers up the back of her graceful neck and into her hair. As my hand slid along her scalp, she leaned back against my chest and turned her head toward me. I caught her chin with my other hand, my eyes falling to her lips, which were open slightly and very inviting.

I stopped myself with my mouth only an inch away from hers. Gods, what was I doing? They'd surely put some kind of spell on me to make me desire her so. It took every ounce of self-restraint I had to release her. I quickly stood up and put some space between us before I could reach for her again.

She opened her eyes and looked at me with obvious disappointment. "Are you okay, Slade?"

"Fine," I said tersely, while trying to gain control of myself again. "That should be enough to help you sleep."

She rose to her feet and straightened her chemise. "Thanks for your help. I'll see you in the morning."

I pointedly looked away, my heart hammering in my chest. "Glad I could be of assistance."

She slipped back into bed and I forced myself to sit back down and look outside again, when all I really wanted to do was crawl in bed beside her. I'd wrap my arms around her and keep her close to me all night, making sure she was safe and happy. I'd gladly do more too, if she wanted it.

I shook my head, disgusted with myself. I'd loved someone once, and I would never go down that path again. Especially not with a woman whose heart would be divided between four of us. I knew where that would lead, and it was nowhere good.

From now on, I had to keep my distance from Kira.

2 2

KIRA

In the morning we had a quick breakfast at the tavern, where I tried to ignore the way Minda looked at Jasin, before we headed to the market to get supplies and some new clothes. We passed by dozens of covered stalls with people yelling about their goods, from stoneware to cloth to fruits and vegetables. Reven, Jasin, and Auric all went separate ways, while Slade stayed by my side for protection, though he didn't say much to me. We'd almost kissed last night and I'd felt a real connection with him finally, but then he'd erected even more walls between us. Now his face was as hard as the stone he could control.

We passed by a stall selling weapons, and Slade took a moment to compliment the owner on their fine craftsmanship. I eyed a sword that would be the perfect size for me, and even held it in my hand briefly to feel its weight, before I put it back and turned away with a heavy heart. I longed for a sword of my own to be able to defend myself better, but I only had a few coins to my name and didn't want to abuse Auric's generosity.

As we continued through the market to pick up the supplies we needed, I tried not to get off track, though it was hard not to be tempted. There were dozens of things I wanted, including some new clothes and a horse, but the more frugal we were now the longer the money would last us.

After Slade and I picked up all the supplies we needed, we found Auric at a stall selling old books, which made me smile. Where else would he be, after all?

"Find anything?" I asked.

Auric closed the book he was flipping through. "Not here, unfortunately. I did get some new clothes, and I bought you a present as well."

He handed me a long, heavy package, and I immediately knew what it was. I tore the paper open and found the sword I'd been looking at earlier. The blade shone under the bright sunlight, while the hilt was simple and black, but it was exactly what I wanted. Auric had also gotten me a new sword belt made of black leather, which I couldn't wait to strap onto my waist.

"Thank you so much," I said to Auric. "But this is too much, really."

"Nonsense. I saw you admiring the sword earlier and knew you had to have it, for your own protection if nothing else." He slid his hand around my waist, drawing me close as his eyes gazed into mine. "If things were different, I'd buy you everything you could ever want. Gowns of the finest silks. Jewels to complement your beauty. An entire library full of books, or a whole arsenal of weapons, if that was more your style. But unfortunately, none of those things are practical right now, so this will have to do."

"I love it." I slid my arms around his neck. "Thank you, Auric."

He brought his lips to mine, while Slade crossed his arms and looked at everything except us. I pulled away from Auric quickly, feeling awkward about kissing one of my mates in front of another. I wasn't sure any of us were ready for that yet.

Slade cleared his throat. "We should get back on the road soon."

We returned to the inn and found Reven waiting outside by the stables, looking impatient and bored. I couldn't tell if he had bought anything or not.

"Have you seen Jasin?" I asked.

"He's upstairs, first door on the right," Reven said, with distaste. "Might want to knock first though."

"Thanks." I headed inside to find our wayward soldier while the other men loaded our supplies onto the horses. The place had cleared out since last night, and I didn't see any sign of Jasin anywhere. My stomach sank as I realized what he must be doing. And with whom.

"Jasin?" I called out, as I rushed up the stairs.

I knocked on the first door, but then threw it open with a burst of anxious energy. Jasin stood inside without a shirt on, while Minda, the waitress from last night, sat on the bed with a smile. My jaw fell open and I could only glance between the two of them, completely speechless. Even though I'd suspected this was what he was doing, it was still so much worse seeing it in person.

"It's not what you think," Jasin said quickly. But I'd already turned on my heel and walked out of the room.

He rushed after me into the hallway, then caught my arm to pull me back to him. He moved close, his naked chest only inches away. Muscles rippled across his skin, showing all the contained strength and power in his body. I swallowed as I forced my gaze up to his face, but that wasn't any better because he was so handsome he made my chest ache. Especially when I thought of him with that other woman.

"Her brother is about my size and I was trading my clothes for his," Jasin said. "Getting rid of my uniform, like you suggested. That was all. Nothing happened, I swear it."

"She was watching you change!"

"I was trying on a shirt to make sure it fit. She saw nothing more than you're seeing now."

I glanced down at his words, taking his body in again. He was so warm I could feel the heat radiating off him, and he smelled good, like a bonfire on a cool night. I had the strongest urge to press myself against him, tilt my head up to his, and ask him to give me some of that warmth too. But then Minda walked out of the room and gave us a smirk before heading down the stairs back to the tavern, and jealousy and hurt rose up in me again. I pulled away.

"Kira?" Jasin asked.

"It's fine," I said. "I just came to tell you we're leaving soon."

"No, it's not." He took my hand and led me into the room, then shut the door behind us. "I can tell you're upset. What can I say or do to make it better?"

"I have no right to be upset. What you do with other women is no business of mine. We've never made any promises to each other and I know you didn't choose this life with me."

His dark eyes were intense and serious as he gazed into mine. "Kira, I'm yours and yours alone. There's nowhere else I'd rather be but by your side."

Gods, how I wanted that to be true, and how I wanted to believe him. But no matter how much I desired him and wanted him for myself, I wasn't sure I could trust him. I pressed my back against the door, my heart racing. "You don't need to say that. You don't even know me."

Jasin placed his hand on the door by my head, leaning close. "I want to know you. In every sense of the word."

A rush of desire flared inside me at his words. He caged me against the wall, and though I could easily step away from him, I didn't dare move. "Me and every other woman, it seems."

"Not anymore. The moment I met you I knew the Fire God had chosen me for a reason, and that reason is you." He used his free hand to cup my face, and I sucked in a breath at his warm touch. "The only woman I want is right in front of me."

"And I'm supposed to believe you'll be loyal? Or happy

with one woman for the rest of your life?" I gazed up at him defiantly, even though he was making me melt. "You admitted you've slept with lots of women."

"I have, yes. But that's all in the past." He arched an eyebrow. "You don't honestly believe the other guys have all been waiting for you to come along, do you? I doubt any of them are strangers to a woman's bed either."

My cheeks flushed. "No, of course not, but you're the one I have to bond with first. And I've never...ah..." I tried to duck my head, embarrassed as soon as the words slipped from my mouth, but he caught my chin and made me look up at him.

"Never?" His eyes flared with obvious desire, and then his gaze dropped to my lips. "Then it's a good thing I'm well versed in the arts of pleasing a woman."

His mouth captured mine, while his strong body pushed me back against the door he leaned against. With dominant hands he tilted my head up to his and gave me the most sensual kiss of my life, teasing a soft moan from my lips. His naked chest pressed against my breasts, and even through my dress I felt how firm his body was. I was suddenly overcome with the need to touch him and placed my hands on his waist, pulling him closer. I needed to claim him as my own in the same way he was claiming me.

His mouth moved to my neck, leaving a trail of light kisses that made me moan again, while my hands smoothed across his hard chest and strong arms. His powerful fighter's body was solid under my fingers, and as his lips skimmed across my collarbone, all I wanted was to feel more of it.

Forget the Fire Temple, I was ready to bond with him right now. Or at least get some of that practice in.

But then he straightened up and stepped back, making me instantly miss his warmth. I nearly pulled him back to me, but somehow regained control of myself. Except there was no denying I'd kissed him back as hard as he'd kissed me. And if he kissed me again? I wouldn't stop him.

He ran his thumb slowly along my lower lip. "That's only a taste of what's to come. But first, I'm going to convince you that the only woman I want is you."

Without another word, he grabbed his clothes off the bed and walked out of the room, still shirtless. Leaving me breathless and dazed and wondering what exactly just happened.

23

KIRA

Another day of travel passed by without incident, except that I was forced to ride with Slade and Reven for long hours while trying to ignore the feel of their strong bodies against mine as they pointedly did not make conversation. I loved my sword, but I really should have asked Auric for my own horse.

At least I wasn't sore anymore. Like my head injury from Roark, my body had recovered quickly from the aches and pains of riding. It made me wonder if my new healing powers were working on myself as well.

After so many days on the road, we were all exhausted by the time we stopped to make camp in the forest. I set my bedroll as far from the fire as possible like I did every night, and both Jasin and Auric rushed to put theirs on either side of mine. Not that Slade or Reven seemed to care about being close to me anyway. Reven was brooding in the shadows as far away from me as possible, and Slade turned away from me when I glanced at him. How was I ever supposed to get close to them if they kept their distance like this?

On the other hand, maybe Slade and Reven were the least of my problems. Jasin and Auric had been glowering at each other all day, and as Jasin walked past me, he bumped into Auric hard and obviously on purpose. Auric muttered a word under his breath that sounded a lot like, "Barbarian."

I couldn't take it anymore. I got to my feet and glared at all of them. "I need a few minutes alone. Don't follow me."

"Stay close," Jasin said.

"I'll be fine," I snapped.

I headed into the dark forest, shoving branches out of my way and kicking at rocks under my boots. But even once I was out of sight, I could still hear their low male voices behind me, though I couldn't make out the words. I moved deeper into the woods, with the bright moon guiding my steps, until I found a large rock to sit upon. I listened carefully. Silence. Blissful, sweet silence.

It was the first time I'd been truly alone with my thoughts for days and I relished it. I'd gotten used to being in solitude for most of my life, and it was hard to adjust to suddenly being around four men all day every day. Even if I enjoyed their presence—when they weren't being obnoxious males, that was. It felt right with all of them at my side, but I realized I still needed some alone time now and then too.

The male voices grew louder, intruding on my quiet moment. Arguing about something, it sounded like. Probably related to me. Maybe I should feel honored they were fighting over me, but I had a feeling it would only get worse as I got closer to each man. Would any of them ever be comfortable sharing me with the others?

Would I?

The idea of sleeping with Jasin didn't make me as nervous as it once did, not after his mind-blowing kiss. But I had also kissed Auric only hours before and enjoyed it just as much. And then there was Slade, who I'd nearly kissed. Not to mention Reven, who I'd definitely *wanted* to kiss, if only because he was so gorgeous in his deadly, dangerous way.

How could I have feelings for all four men? It didn't make sense. Lust, I could understand. Friendship as well. But I felt more than that for all of them. Not love, not yet, but the potential that I could love each of them someday. It had to be the magical bond pulling us together and nothing more, right?

I covered my face in my hands, feeling overwhelmed by it all. That's when I heard something moving in the bushes near me.

I jumped to my feet and rested my hand on the hilt of my sword as I scanned the woods. Something was out there.

I was about to call the guys, when the leaves swept aside and the old woman I'd met on my birthday stepped forward.

"Hello there," she said, as if it was perfectly normal for her to run into me in the middle of the nowhere. "Kira, isn't it?"

"You," I said, my mouth hanging open. "Are you the Spirit Goddess?"

She let out a low laugh. "Gods, no. Why would you think that?"

My heart sank and I sighed. "You were outside Stoneham on my birthday, and now you're here. How?"

The old woman shrugged. "I get around."

"Are you following me?" I asked, my eyes narrowing.

"Not exactly."

She settled in on a rock opposite mine and I slowly sat back down since I sensed she wasn't a threat. She looked exactly as I'd seen her before, down to the same hooded robe. How had she wound up here, in the middle of the woods? We weren't anywhere near a town this time and she was alone, without even a horse.

"You can call me Enva," she said, as she folded her hands in her lap. "Let's just say I have a special interest in you."

"Do you know who—what—I am?"

"I do, and I might be able to help you." She cocked her head. "I'm sure you have some questions."

"Hundreds of them," I said. "Is it true? Am I the next Black Dragon?"

"Yes, you are. Assuming you live long enough to claim that title." She shrugged. "None of the others have ever made it that far."

My mouth dropped open. "There were others?"

"Of course," she said, as if it were obvious. "You didn't think you and Nysa were the only ones, did you?"

Nysa, the Black Dragon. Even hearing her name sent shivers down my spine. "I wasn't sure. I've never heard of any others."

"Because she kills them all before they become a threat."

I swallowed the lump in my throat. "But not me."

"She doesn't know about you. Yet. Best thing to do is to keep it that way as long as you can."

I nodded slowly. "We'll do our best."

"See that you do." Enva examined her fingernails on one of her wrinkled hands. "Any other questions? I don't have all evening."

She was mighty pushy, considering she was the one who'd visited me. "Why did the Gods choose me?"

She let out a sharp laugh. "They didn't."

I blinked at her. "I...I don't understand."

"The others were chosen. You were born."

My mouth fell open as I absorbed this bit of information. "How?"

She gave me a sardonic look. "I'm pretty sure you know how that happens. I should hope so, or you're going to be in for a big surprise when you reach the Fire Temple."

I bit back a frustrated response and asked, "Did my parents know about what I was?"

"Yes."

I nodded slowly as everything I knew about my past realigned. The Dragons had been looking for me all along. My parents really were killed because of me. "But there was never anything special about me. I never had any powers or anything. Not until now."

"Animals have always been drawn to you. You've always had a way with plants and herbs as well. Those are all gifts from the Spirit Goddess."

"What about the healing? That only started recently."

She nodded. "You came into your powers on your twentieth birthday, although you still have a long way to go. After you bond with your mates you'll be able to take on their powers as well." With those words she stood up. "I think that's enough for one night. I'm sure we'll meet again. If you live that long."

She gave me a short nod before stepping back into the forest. I called out, "Wait!" but she had already disappeared. Literally. Leaving me with a few answers, and even more questions than before.

24

KIRA

When I returned to camp I told the guys about my strange visit from Enva, but none of them had any further insight into what she'd said or who she was. For now, she remained a mystery.

And thanks to her, I was stuck with four overprotective men who kept telling me not to wander off by myself again. The tension between them was still there, but they were united under a new purpose: keeping an eye on me at all times. Needless to say, I wasn't thrilled.

"Where are you going?" Slade asked me the next morning, as I walked toward the forest. He was already jumping to his feet and grabbing his axe as if to follow me.

I gave him an exasperated look. "I need to relieve myself. Could I get a tiny bit of privacy?"

Jasin looked up from where he was sharpening his sword. "You shouldn't go anywhere alone."

"For once I agree with Jasin," Auric said. He was jotting notes down in his journal, likely recording everything that had happened yesterday. "One of us should be with you at all times."

I propped my hands on my hips. "Seriously, I'm fine. First of all, I wasn't even in any danger last night, and second of all, I can protect myself."

"We know you can, but it's our duty to protect you," Slade said, his brow furrowing.

Auric nodded. "Exactly. We don't know who or what Enva was. Your encounter with her proves there are forces at work we don't understand, whose interests might not be aligned with ours. We won't know until we learn more."

"Don't follow me. I mean it!" I snapped, before storming into the forest without looking back to see if they listened. If my infuriating men wanted to chase after me, that was their problem. I couldn't live my entire life making sure one of them was guarding me at all times.

I took care of my business quickly, just in case they *were* watching, then headed back toward camp. I caught sight of Reven standing in front of a stream, making the water rise and fall in front of him, almost like it was dancing.

I sighed. "Did they send you to keep an eye on me?"

"Hardly." The water stopped moving immediately as he turned toward me with a scowl.

I gestured toward the stream. "Good to see you're practicing. You should train with the others too sometime."

He gave me a scathing look. "No thanks. I have no interest in keeping these powers."

139

I blinked at him. "Are you still planning to leave?"

"I am."

I'd thought he had changed his mind after all we'd been through. And with everything else already frustrating me, this was the last straw. I gestured into the forest angrily. "Why don't you go then? No one's stopping you."

"None of you would survive a day without me." He shook his head with disdain. "Besides, I can't leave. The Gods saw to that. But I'll find a way."

"Good luck with that," I tossed over my shoulder as I stomped off through the woods, even more annoyed than I'd been before. I didn't even glance at the other men when I entered camp again, just grabbed my bow and quiver and stalked back into the forest. Target practice. That's what I needed.

Once I was in place, I pulled the bow taut and released an arrow. It flew true and struck the tree in exactly the spot I'd intended, a little round knot in the trunk. As the arrow vibrated against the wood, I drew another one and prepared to shoot again.

"Not bad," Jasin said, as he approached me through the trees.

I arched an eyebrow at him, then released my arrow without even looking at my target. It struck the tree in nearly the same spot. "Not bad?"

"You're definitely good, I'll give you that."

"You think you can do better?" I asked.

With a cocky smile, he pulled his own bow off his back

and drew an arrow. With lightning fast movements, he fired into the tree, his own red-tipped arrow nearly on top of mine. As I watched, he fired three more times, forming a circle around my own arrows. What a show off.

Not to be outdone, I released my own volley, splitting each one of his arrows in half with my own. I turned to him with a wry smile.

"Let's call it a draw," he said, with a wink.

"If you insist," I said, shaking my head.

He gestured at my waist. "How's that new sword? You any good with it?"

"Getting there." I put my bow down on a tall rock and drew my blade. It fit perfectly in my hand and the weight was ideal for my size, although it was much smaller than Jasin's.

He drew his own sword. "Let's see what you've got."

I lunged for him, but he was fast, even with his heavier weapon. Our blades clashed, the ringing of metal echoing through the forest as we exchanged blows. I was sure he was holding back, especially knowing how strong he was, but it was good practice for me anyway. And as we fought, my tension and frustration slowly melted away.

"You favor your right side," he said. "Be careful of that."

I nodded and made a mental adjustment, then slashed out at him. He did a quick swirling maneuver and the next thing I knew my sword was sticking out of the ground a few feet away. Then he grabbed me from behind, his free arm across my chest, holding me tight against him. I nearly fought back, but then his lips were on my neck, and all the fight left me.

"So easy to let down your guard?" he asked, as his teeth nipped at my earlobe. "Or maybe you wanted me to catch you?"

I stomped on his foot and pushed away from him, but all he did was laugh. Breathing heavily, I used his moment of distraction to knock his sword away. Then we were fighting hand to hand, blocking each other's blows, although he was so much more experienced than I was that it was hardly a fair fight.

He knocked me off my feet, but I brought him down with me onto the forest floor. We tumbled over until I found myself on top of him, staring down at him as he laughed again.

"If you wanted to get on top of me, there are easier ways," he said, as his hands rested on my waist.

I gazed into his eyes, my heart beating fast, and not just from our fight. "Don't read too much into this."

"No? This is the second time we've been on the ground together. Although last time I was on top. You'll have to tell me which position you prefer."

I pushed on his chest to stand up, but he caught my wrists and pulled me back to him. The anger from before quickly turned to passion as our mouths found each other for a smoldering kiss. All I could think about was his firm body beneath mine and the way his arms circled my back to hold me against him like he never wanted to let go.

"Kira?" Auric called out from somewhere in the distance.

Jasin broke off our kiss and released me. "As much as I'd like to continue this, I think our companions are calling us."

Reality came crashing back in and I sat up, feeling dazed. I brushed leaves off myself. "Right. We should get going."

Jasin rose to his feet and offered me a hand, then pulled me close for one more kiss. "We'll continue this later."

The other three men were already on their horses and gave us looks that showed they knew exactly what we were doing. I tried not to let it get to me. Jasin would be the first to have me, and there was nothing I could do about that. Only Auric was even trying to stake his claim, so what did Slade and Reven have to be upset about?

I decided to ride with Slade, hoping it would stop some of the jealous looks. As usual, his quiet, calm strength made me feel better, as if just being near him soothed all the anxious thoughts swirling in my mind. I also found it easy to talk to him, much more so than any of the others.

"Slade, is there a magical bond tying you to me now? Or could you leave if you wanted?" I asked, as I remembered Reven's words.

"I don't know," he said, in that low, grumbly voice I found so sexy. "Originally, we had this overwhelming urge to find you, but that passed once we met. I suspect any of us could leave now, but maybe not after we're officially bound together."

I nodded slowly. If Slade was right, then Reven could have left at any time. He was simply using the magic as an excuse. Maybe a tiny part of him wanted to be here after all.

As we rode, the landscape began to change. The forest thinned out around us, the trees becoming sparse and the ground becoming harder. I'd heard much of the Air Realm was a desert, but we wouldn't go very far into it, luckily. At least not yet.

To avoid the border crossing—where the Onyx Guard soldiers might give us trouble—Jasin had us go out of our way over some steep hills that our horses were not happy about in the slightest. The off-road terrain slowed us down and it felt like we were making no progress at all, until we were officially in the Air Realm.

Slade's horse threw a shoe only a few minutes later, and we were forced to stop at the first village we found. None of us thought it was safe to do so, but we didn't have much choice, and luckily the place was small enough that there were few soldiers in it. Slade immediately took the horse to the local blacksmith, while the rest of us went to find rooms for the evening.

The inn was mostly empty and much smaller than the one we'd stayed in the other night, which suited us fine. The fewer people who saw us, the better.

"We'd like a room for the evening," Jasin said to the innkeeper, a stout man with a moustache.

"Of course. We have many rooms available. How many will you need?"

Jasin glanced back at Auric, who said, "Two, I think."

The innkeeper nodded as he scanned our group. But then he paused and his eyes widened. He suddenly dropped to one knee, bowing his head. "Your highness! I'm sorry, I didn't recognize you at first. Please forgive me, Prince Tanariel."

I stared at him in confusion, until I realized who he was addressing.

Auric.

25

AURIC

I knew we should never have stopped in the Air Realm.

I cleared my throat, trying not to show my panic. "You must be mistaken. I'm not Prince Tanariel, I simply bear a passing resemblance to him. Please stand up."

The innkeeper slowly rose to his feet and lowered his voice. "Of course. Your secret is safe with me, your highness."

I pinched the bridge of my nose. "Please don't call me that."

"My apologies." He clapped his hands together and smiled at the group. "Now then. You'll have the finest rooms available, and I'll make sure some food and wine is brought up for you. Is there anything else I can do for you?"

"That will be great, thanks," Jasin said, as he glared at me. He already hated me, and now he had even more reason. Not that I was particularly fond of him either, but I didn't want to fight with him, for Kira's sake at least.

And Kira... she gaped at me like she'd never seen me before. My gut twisted with guilt and shame from deceiving her, even if I had a good reason for keeping my identity hidden. Now that my secret was out, would she look at me differently, knowing who I truly was?

The innkeeper showed us to two of his best rooms, which meant they were slightly larger and cleaner than the others, before apologizing again and promising to have someone bring up some refreshments. I pressed a coin into his hand and assured him all was well.

The second he was gone, Kira turned to me with narrowed eyes and asked, "You're a prince? I thought you said you were only a distant relation!"

I sighed. "I said I was no one of consequence in the family, which is true."

"I don't think being fifth in line to the throne of the Air Realm counts as inconsequential," she snapped.

"I can explain everything," I said quickly.

"Better get started, Auric," Jasin said, crossing his arms. "Or should we call you Prince Tanariel? Is Auric even your name?"

I pinched the bridge of my nose. "It's my middle name. No one calls me Tanariel. That was my grandfather, not me."

"So you really are a prince," Kira said.

I met her eyes. "Yes, I am."

"I'm surprised none of you recognized him," Reven said from the corner, where he was flipping one of his knives.

"You knew who he was all along?" Kira asked, growing visibly more upset. "And you never thought to mention he was a prince at any point?"

Reven shrugged. "Not my problem."

"It's all of our problems," Jasin said. "Auric was going to be recognized sooner or later, which puts all of us at risk. He should have told us long before we got to the Air Realm."

"Yes, he should have," Kira said.

Before I could respond she threw open the door and stomped out. Silently cursing myself for being an idiot, I started to follow after her, but Slade blocked me in the doorway.

"What's going on?" he asked, sounding weary.

"Auric is a prince of the Air Realm," Jasin explained in a low growl.

Without waiting for Slade's response, I darted after Kira, who had slipped into the other bedroom reserved for us. I closed the door behind me and faced her. "Kira, I know you're upset, and you have every right to be. But please let me try to explain."

"You lied to me," she said, in a way that made my heart twist.

"I didn't lie, not once. Everything I told you was true, I simply...omitted certain things."

She sat down on the edge of one of the beds. "Some really big things. Things you should have told me."

I sat beside her. "Probably, yes. But you have to understand that when this started I had no idea who you or the others were. I didn't know if I could trust any of you. Telling people I'm a prince is like putting a target on my back. Not to mention, people treat me differently once they know who —what—I am. I didn't want that to happen with you, Kira. I wanted you to get to know me as you would any other man, not as a prince. And after everyone's reaction to me being a nobleman, can you blame me for being hesitant to reveal the truth?"

"I understand why you didn't tell me at first, but don't you trust me now?" she asked.

"I do, yes. And I was going to tell you at the right moment, I promise."

She raised an eyebrow. "When was that going to be?"

"Um." I swallowed the lump in my throat. "Before we reached the Air Temple, for sure."

She sighed. "I just don't know how I can trust you anymore."

"I'm sorry I kept this from you, but please try to understand. I'm the youngest prince, with enough older siblings to make sure I'll never be king. In my family, I'm the odd one out who was always in the library instead of attending balls and dealing with politics. I never cared about any of that and so to them I've always been inconsequential. So yes, I am a prince, but at the same time, nothing about me has changed."

She nodded slowly. "Are you hiding anything else from me?"

"Not exactly," I said. "There's nothing I am *hiding.*

Simply things I haven't chosen to share yet. Surely you can understand that. There are lots of things you haven't told us either, and I don't see you getting upset with Reven for not sharing all the details of his past. But in time, I'll be willing to open up completely."

She blew out a breath. "Okay, I see your point."

"Thank you. I truly had no wish to deceive you, I just wanted to make sure my place in the group was more stable before I told everyone."

"Why wouldn't it be stable?"

I cleared my throat and looked away. "I've been reminded many times that I don't fit in with the rest of you."

"Ignore the others." She leaned against my side. "I want you to stay, and that's all that matters."

"You do?" I took her hand in mine. "Because I have no desire to leave either. This is my life now." I slowly ran my thumbs along her knuckles. "That's another reason I didn't mention I was a prince. In my mind, I no longer am one. I gave up that life and that title when I left home to find you."

"Do you regret leaving all of that behind?"

"Not one bit. I'm your mate and one day I'll be the Golden Dragon. That is more than I ever dreamed of, and all I could ever want."

She melted into my embrace and our lips found each other easily. Kissing Kira was the most amazing thing I'd ever experienced. When we touched, sparks danced between us, but when we kissed, our connection flashed like a burst of lightning. I could only imagine what it would be like after we'd officially bonded.

Her hand rested on my thigh as she moved even closer, and the sensation shot straight to my groin. I groaned as I pulled her flush against me, my fingers digging into her hips as I took the kiss deeper. This woman, Gods. She was gorgeous, but that wasn't why I cared for her so much already. It was her intelligence, her kindness, and her inner strength that had won me over. Even now, she accepted me for who I truly was, despite my mistake of not telling her the truth sooner. How had I gotten so lucky to end up as one of her mates? When I met the Air God again, I'd be sure to thank him for choosing me.

Her hands stroked my jaw, but she finally pulled away. "Come on. Let's go calm the others down."

When we went into the other room, she held my hand, even though the other men eyed me warily. "All right," Kira said, as she glanced between them. "Auric was a prince once, but he's one of us now, and that's all that matters."

Jasin frowned and looked away, while Reven shrugged as if he couldn't care less. Slade said, "Fine with me."

"I know this isn't easy for any of us, and I can't expect all of you to get along, but please try at least." She looked between me and Jasin. "For me."

"Fine," he muttered.

"Of course," I said, squeezing her hand.

A knock sounded on the door, and the innkeeper and a young woman brought in large trays of food with two bottles of wine. If nothing else, at least we'd be well fed tonight. I still wasn't thrilled my true identity had been revealed this way, but at least the weight had been lifted off my shoulders and I didn't have to keep it from Kira anymore. Of course, once we got closer to the Air Temple, I'd have to reveal some of the other things I was afraid to admit—but hopefully she would accept those parts of me too.

26

KIRA

As we continued through the rolling hills of the Air Realm, passing a few farms but little else, I thought back on what had happened the night before. Auric was a *prince*. Even now it was hard to wrap my head around the idea. It was even harder to accept that he had given all that up to be with me.

I wasn't happy that he'd kept something this huge from me, but I also didn't blame him. I understood his reasons, even if I didn't like them. And it's not like the other guys were all that forthright about their pasts either. Nor was I, for that matter. But I was beginning to think the only way we'd get through this was if we started trusting each other.

Easier said than done, of course.

My thoughts were interrupted when I began to smell smoke. We were moving through a large field of wheat, and I noticed black smoke rising in the distance to our left. A bonfire? I hoped that was all it was, but we didn't really have time to stop, especially when it was probably nothing.

A piercing, inhuman shriek tore through the air, one I hadn't heard in seven years. I was suddenly doused in pure terror, as if a bucket of ice water had been dumped over my head. My arms tightened around Reven's chest as he pulled our horse to a stop and reached for one of his knives.

"What was that?" Auric asked.

"A Dragon," I whispered.

Then it appeared. Through the black smoke, the beast rose up on his giant, blood red wings. Sark, the Crimson Dragon. The monster who had haunted my nightmares for much of my life.

The others tensed, but there was nowhere we could run —we were out in the open, too far from anywhere we could hide. If we had to fight Sark with our weapons and our magic, would we even stand a chance?

But Sark didn't even glance our way. With a great flap of wings that sent the smoke billowing away, he cast one last breath of fire on whatever was below him before flying off toward the west, his tail whipping behind him. Within seconds, he was only a dark speck in the sky, and then he was gone.

Reven suddenly kicked his horse into action and charged us forward, toward the smoke. I was torn between telling him to run the opposite direction and yelling for him to hurry. The others followed right at our heels as we made it through the wheat field and burst out onto a farm. The smoke was stronger here, and soon I spotted flames flickering up ahead.

A small house in the middle of the farm was completely on fire. Many of the flames had already begun to spread to the surrounding fields as well. Reven immediately summoned water and doused the field to stop it from being engulfed, then leaped off his horse and called forth even more water to work on the house.

I tumbled off the horse as well, but all I could do was stare at the flames in horror. There was no screaming, but the air smelled of burnt flesh, just as it had when I was a child. I was trapped inside my bleakest memory and my worst nightmare and there was no escape.

When the others arrived, I could only wrap my arms around myself and shake as they tried to stop the fire too. Jasin managed the flames as best he could and tried to coax them to die down. Auric calmed the wind and sucked the air from the fire. Slade covered the house in dirt and soil. But it was Reven who did the most, as he called down wave after wave to douse the raging inferno.

I wished there was something more I could do, but at the same time I was relieved that I didn't have to get any closer. Seeing this happen again was bad enough. Getting near the flames would have been impossible. Even standing at a safe distance, I was trembling and struggling to breathe, and not just from the smoke. How was I supposed to bond with Jasin, knowing it would turn him into a dragon like Sark? Or that it would give me these dark powers too?

I wasn't sure how long it took for the men to put out the

fire, but it seemed like an eternity. By the time they were done, the house was little more than a charcoal ruin, and if anyone had been inside, there was no way they could have survived. Bile rose up in my throat at the thought of charred, blackened bodies, like my parents had once become. No matter how hard I tried, I would never be able to scrub that image from my brain.

One by one the men returned to my side, all of them covered in black soot with sweat running down their faces, looking as haunted as I felt.

"Why would he do this?" Auric asked with a weary voice.

Slade leaned against his horse and wiped his face. "This is what the Dragons do to anyone suspected of being in the Resistance."

"Were there people inside?" I asked, though I almost didn't want to know the answer.

Jasin dropped his head. "We were too late to save them."

I nodded, as tears pricked my eyes. I tried to blink them away, but it was no use. Another family had been snuffed out by Sark. Jasin moved close and tried to wrap an arm around me, but I pushed him away.

"Don't touch me," I said, stepping back. "You're going to be the Crimson Dragon soon. The same as him."

"I'm nothing like Sark," Jasin said in a rush. "You have to know that."

I shook my head. I knew I wasn't making sense, but all I could think about was Jasin summoning flames like Sark. Flames which could be used to destroy lives, like they had done today. Like they had done to my family all those years ago.

"Just leave me alone," I said, as I stumbled into the wheat field.

Memories of my family's death crowded my head as I ran. The flames. The screams. The smells. Oh Gods, the smells. The same smells that lingered in the air now.

I had to get away.

27

REVEN

"**I**'m going after her," Jasin said, already charging forth into the field.

Slade caught the soldier's shoulder. "Don't. You're the last person she wants to see right now."

Jasin's brow furrowed. "But why? I'm not the one who set that house on fire. I would never do anything like that!"

"She knows that, but she's not thinking clearly right now. Just give her some space."

"Fine," Jasin said, slumping against a broken cart. "I just hate seeing her upset."

"We all do," Auric said.

While they stood around moping, I slipped between the trees, needing space of my own. Like Kira, the sight and smell of that fire, plus that cursed dragon in the sky, had brought back a lot of painful memories. Now I wanted nothing more than to get away from this place and wash the soot and ash off my hands and clothes.

I'd tried my best to put out the fire. I'd done what I could to save the people inside. But I'd failed. Just like I'd failed when I was a child and couldn't save my family from Sark's fire. Except now it was worse, because I could summon water. But my magic still wasn't enough.

It was a stark reminder that I shouldn't be here. I was no hero. Most of my life I'd been a villain. That wasn't going to change. The sooner I left, the better it would be for everyone.

I spotted Kira ahead of me, crumpled on the ground, and found myself making my way over to her even though I knew it was a bad idea. Not only because she needed some space, but because I didn't want to get involved with her. I had to keep my distance so I could easily leave when the time came. But I couldn't ignore the sight of her back hunched over in the dirt, knowing she was in as much pain as I was.

She looked up with a start as I emerged from the wheat beside her, then let out a sad laugh. "You're the last person I would have expected to come find me."

I crossed my arms. "Don't get the wrong idea. I'm not here to comfort you."

She wiped at her eyes. "Then why are you here?"

"I couldn't stand to listen to your boyfriends bicker anymore so I went for a walk. I just happened to stumble across you here."

"I see," she said, although she didn't sound convinced. She was no longer crying though, and instead regarded me with a curious expression on her face. "You could have kept walking."

I gave a casual shrug. "I like this spot."

The slightest hint of a smile crossed her lips. "Me too."

For the next few minutes she wiped at her soot-streaked face and stared off into the fields, while her breathing slowed and her shoulders relaxed. I stood near her in companionable silence, though I had to fight the urge to wrap my arms around her and tell her everything would be okay. She didn't need my pity or my comfort, anyway. She was already strong and brave and didn't want someone to save her. She simply needed a few moments to remember all that.

When she rose to her feet, she was steady again. "Thank you."

"For what?" I asked.

"For being here with me." She moved close and pressed a hand against my black leather jerkin, looking up at me with those intriguing eyes. "For letting me have a moment to calm down while still showing me I wasn't alone."

"You're reading way too much into my actions." I should really move away. I didn't.

"Maybe so," she said, but then she slid her arms around my chest.

My entire body stiffened at her touch. It took me a moment to realize she was *hugging* me, of all things. Gods, when was the last time someone had hugged me? I couldn't even remember. Was it my parents, before the Crimson Dragon had taken them from me? Or was it Mara, before she was killed?

My throat grew tight as emotions I tried to keep tramped down suddenly flooded me. My grief and pain at seeing the burning house and the Crimson Dragon must mirror Kira's own, and maybe on some level she sensed that. Though I couldn't talk about it, and wasn't sure I would ever be able to, I understood more than anyone what she was going through.

My arms came up of their own will and circled her, pulling her tighter against my chest. She breathed out a light sigh and softened into my embrace, resting her head on my shoulder. Time melted away as we held each other, and a terrible yearning filled me as I slowly ran my fingers through her hair. For a few seconds, I imagined what it would be like if I let myself become one of her mates and could hold her like this anytime.

Startled by that train of thought, I pulled away abruptly and stepped back to put some distance between us. I'd let myself feel too much, but that was over now. I locked all those emotions away in the dark recesses of my mind, until I was calm and cool again, like ice.

"We should head back before your boyfriends start to miss you," I said.

I turned away and began walking toward the others before she could open her mouth and make me stay with the slightest word. She made me feel too much, and that was dangerous. Caring for people made you vulnerable, and emotions made you weak.

I knew that all too well.

28

KIRA

On our seventh day of traveling we finally made it to
the Fire Realm.

According to Jasin, there was no way to avoid the border
crossing here. This part of the Fire Realm was walled off as
far as the eye could see, and the only way through was at one
of the gates, which were all manned by the Onyx Army.

Jasin donned his black and red uniform, which he still
had packed away, and led us to the gate. Onyx Army
soldiers in full armor with red markings on their shoulders
scrutinized us as we approached. Archers stood on the walls,
ready to strike us down if we made a run for it.

A soldier wearing a helmet with red dragon wings on it
stepped forward and held up a hand for us to stop. "What is
your business in the Fire Realm?" he called out.

"I'm escorting these people to Ashbury," Jasin said.

The soldier removed his helmet. "Jasin, is that you?"

"Gregil?" Jasin flashed him a smile. "Good to see you. What are you doing out here?"

The soldier chuckled softly. "Stuck on border duty for this quarter. You know how it goes."

"That I do." He gestured to the rest of us. "I'm just taking some friends and family to Ashbury to visit my parents."

Gregil nodded. "That shouldn't be a problem, although we need to search through your things."

Jasin groaned. "Do you really? We're in a bit of a rush, and you know me, after all."

"Sorry, General's orders. Shouldn't take long."

We were asked to dismount and step aside, while four soldiers took our horses and began going through all of our things. Every muscle in my body turned into a tight knot as I watched them, though I couldn't think of anything suspicious we might be carrying. As they searched, Jasin moved to the side to speak quietly with Gregil. Reven crossed his arms and pretended not to care, but I sensed a tension in him, as if he could snap into action at a moment's notice. Auric looked worried, and I wondered if he was scared they might find his journal. Slade, on the other hand, seemed far too calm considering the situation.

"You sure have a lot of weapons for ordinary travelers," a female soldier said, giving us a suspicious look.

"Can't be too careful these days," Slade said casually. "There are bandits everywhere. Especially in the Earth Realm."

She sniffed. "Maybe so. In the Fire Realm we take care of threats like that so our roads are safe."

Slade smiled at her like they were good friends. "So I've heard. Hence why I'm moving here."

The soldier nodded at that as if it made perfect sense and continued her search, but her suspicions seemed to have eased thanks to Slade. But as we waited, I heard someone shout behind us, and a man yell, "No, please!"

I turned toward the sound, where a young man was being dragged off a horse by another soldier. The man cried out again, but the sound cut short when the soldier thrust a sword into his throat. My eyes bulged and my own hand went to my neck in response. I'd heard the Onyx Army was especially brutal in the Fire Realm, like the Dragon they served, but it was different witnessing it in person.

"A thief," the female soldier said. "Got what he deserved."

"Naturally," Slade said, though his voice had shifted, becoming harder.

As the man's blood stained the road beneath us, I forced myself to turn away. There was nothing we could do for him. Even if we'd tried to help, that would only have gotten us killed too. But knowing that was little comfort.

When they finally let us go, we mounted our horses again and were allowed to move through the gates. On the other side I saw all the preparations to defend against elementals, but also spotted more dried blood and smelled a whiff of death. I could only relax again once the gate was far behind us.

The land here was flat, with great plains that spread as far as the eye could see and an endless sky full of large, fluffy clouds. Far in the distance I could barely make out the mountains where we were headed. The Fire Temple was located at a large volcano on the other side of those tall peaks, and Auric estimated we should be there in two more days.

None of us knew what to expect when we reached the temples. Though the Gods were still worshipped in theory, most people had forgotten about them over the years, and instead had begun to worship and fear the Dragons. We knew the Dragons got their powers from the Gods, but the Gods were distant and immaterial, while the Dragons were things we could see, hear, and fear. Few people made the pilgrimage to the five temples anymore, though Auric said that there were still priests tending to each one. Hopefully they would be able to give us a little more guidance or offer some much-needed answers.

As we approached the mountains, the plains turned rockier and the sky turned dark with thick, black clouds. I pulled my hood over my head just as rain began to fall. The spring shower was cool and refreshing after a long day of travel, until it turned into a heavy downpour that soaked us all through.

"I thought the Fire Realm would be warmer," Slade muttered, from where he sat in front of me.

"We need to get out of this," Auric said. "We should make for the town at the base of the mountains."

Jasin frowned as he glanced in the direction of the town.

"That's Ashbury. Not a good idea. Someone might recognize me there. Plus, it's a pretty large city, second only to the capital of the Fire Realm, Flamedale."

Auric spread his hands. "We can't exactly camp out in this."

Jasin snorted. "Sure we can. What, not good enough for a prince?"

Auric glared at Jasin, while the rain continued to pummel us. The only one who didn't seem to mind it was Reven, who somehow remained dry through it all, like the water simply flowed around him. Having his powers would definitely come in handy right now.

"It wouldn't hurt to get supplies and a decent night's sleep before we set off for the Fire Temple," I said.

"More supplies?" Reven asked skeptically.

"Food, specifically. You guys eat as much as a small village. We're going to need a lot of it since Jasin says the land around the volcano is basically inhospitable."

Slade dismounted and placed his hand flat on the ground. When he straightened up, he shook his head. "There's no other shelter around here."

"To Ashbury it is," I said.

We ducked our heads and headed deeper into the storm with the promise of a hot meal and a warm bed urging us on. None of us spoke as our horses plowed through the storm, as eager to get out of it as we were.

By the time we got to Ashbury my clothes were completely soaked through. This city was one of the larger ones I'd seen and had a massive stone wall around it, along with a wide moat and fiery brazier burning bright every few feet, even in this downpour. Not to mention, a whole lot of soldiers.

By some luck, the guards—who looked as miserable as we were to be out in the rain—waved us through the gate without even inspecting us. I tensed as we passed through the metal entry, worried we'd encounter some trouble, but we made it into Ashbury without incident. The city was full of great stone structures with pointed, sharp architecture, but the streets were nearly empty at the moment.

As soon as we made it fully inside the town's walls, the rain fizzled out.

"Figures," Jasin said. "Should we keep going or stop here?"

"I'm not sure," Auric said.

"It could start up again at any moment," Reven said, gazing at the sky.

"Not sure about you, but I trust the water guy," Slade said.

"Let's stop," I said. It was still early and we were making today's progress even slower, but if it started pouring again we would be caught in it. Besides, we really did need more food—I couldn't believe how much these four men ate.

We found a quiet inn that wasn't on a main road where we could stop for the night and not draw too much attention. We left our horses there, but it was too early to eat or sleep, so we decided to do our shopping now while the sun was returning to the sky and the city was slowly drying off.

We headed for the market, but were slowed by a large

crowd forming around a raised platform in what appeared to be the town square. Soldiers in black scaled armor stood watch around the fringes of the crowd, while more walked out onto the stage. Jasin pulled his hood low over his head as we moved between the people looking at whatever was about to happen.

"What's going on?" I asked, straining to see over the crowd around us.

Reven met my eyes, his face grim. "An execution is about to begin."

My stomach dropped out from under me at Reven's words. As I stared at the platform, I noticed something I'd first missed—a large pyre. They were going to burn someone alive. But who were they executing and why?

Jasin's eyes darted around, his hand resting on his sword. "We should get out of here."

"I agree," Slade said. "Kira shouldn't be here for this."

A huge man stepped onto the platform and loomed over the crowd in his shining armor, the large dragon wings on his helmet flashing under the sun. Unlike the other soldiers, his armor and helmet were blood red.

Jasin swore under his breath. "That's General Voor."

"You know him?" I asked.

"I served under him for two years." He gripped my arm. "We really need to go. Now."

Auric glanced at the soldiers around the edges of the

crowd. "It's too late. If we run out of here now it will be suspicious."

On the platform soldiers began dragging out a row of people who were all tied together in a line. They stumbled forward, at least ten of them, both men and women, young and old. One of them couldn't be more than twelve or thirteen, while another looked closer to her sixties.

"These people have all been found guilty of being part of the Resistance," General Voor called out, his voice oddly metallic from behind his helmet. "By order of the Black Dragon they will pay for their crimes. With fire."

I watched in horror as each prisoner was moved toward the pyre and tied to stakes rising out of it. The young boy stumbled and fell, and a woman I assumed was his mother jerked toward him to help. A soldier pushed her back hard, while another one roughly shoved the child toward the fire pit. The crowd remained hushed the entire time, although I caught a few people silently crying into their hands, while others nodded in support at the General. The soldiers glared at us from the sidelines the entire time, ready to step in if anyone got out of line.

"We have to help them," I blurted out, surprising even myself.

"We can't," Jasin set, his jaw clenched. "I don't like this any more than you do, but if we get involved we'll only put ourselves in danger."

"But we have to do something!"

"We can't. We'll expose who we are and likely get ourselves killed in the process."

"I'm with Jasin," Reven said. "We need to stay out of this and lay low. Besides, it's not our fight."

"Of course it is!" I turned to Slade and Auric. "Surely you don't also think we should just stand here and watch these people die?"

Slade stroked his beard slowly as he considered. "I agree we should help them, but only if we can get you out safely first."

I huffed. "I'm not going anywhere."

His green eyes met mine. "Kira, I don't like this any more than you do, but my responsibility is to protect you first."

"I'm going to help them whether you join me or not. So if you want to protect me, I suggest you stick by my side."

Auric eyed the platform as if it were a puzzle to solve. "Is there a way to rescue them while making sure we all get out alive and don't reveal our powers?"

"I don't know," I said. "But this is why we were given these powers. To stop the Black Dragon and her followers."

Jasin ran a ragged hand through his short, damp hair. "Maybe so, but we're not strong enough yet, and there are too many soldiers. And trust me, we do not want to get General Voor's attention. "

"We need to create a diversion," Auric said. "Jasin can set something on fire to distract the soldiers, and then we'll go in."

"This is a really bad idea," Reven muttered.

I gave him a sharp look. "Then come up with a better one, because we're doing this with or without your help."

"Fine." Jasin glanced around, as if checking where we were. "This city has underground tunnels that the Resistance use to get around. There's an entrance behind that shop over there."

"Where do the tunnels go?" Reven asked.

"To different parts of the city, but also beyond the walls."

"How do you know all this?" Auric asked.

Jasin hesitated. "That doesn't matter right now."

Determination crackled within me as the plan came together in my head. "So we distract the guards, free the prisoners, and get them to the tunnels, where we should be able to escape?"

"Exactly," Jasin said.

"Oh, is that all?" Reven asked sardonically, shaking his head.

"Are you sure you want to do this?" Slade asked me.

I swallowed and glanced at the prisoners on the platform, who were now all tied to the stakes and awaiting their fate. All my life I'd stayed out of trouble and kept my head down in order to survive. I'd never wanted to fight for a cause or overthrow an empire, I'd just wanted to survive another day. But if I was supposed to save the world from the Black Dragon, I couldn't hide in the shadows forever. Not if I wanted to fight for what was right.

My back straightened with resolve. "Yes, I'm sure. The Gods chose us so we could bring balance back to the world. It's time we started doing that."

"If we're going to do this, we need to hurry," Slade said, his face grim. "They're lighting the pyres now."

"Cover your faces and get to the prisoners. I'll cause a distraction." Jasin ripped some fabric off his shirt sleeve and tied it around his face to cover everything below his nose. Then he raised his hood again, so that all I could see were his eyes.

I wrapped my arms around him and gave him a quick squeeze. "Be careful."

He rested his forehead against mine briefly. "You too."

"We'll keep her safe," Slade said, resting a hand on my back.

Jasin gave him a nod, before slipping into the crowd. We covered our faces like he'd done and started toward the stage, weaving around the people in front of us.

Someone shouted as an empty cart in the middle of the crowd went up in flames. Panic spiked in my chest, even though I knew it was Jasin's distraction, and I forced myself to stay calm. People around us began screaming and pushing to get away from the fire, while soldiers rushed forward to investigate. I prayed Jasin could get away safely.

Unfortunately, the soldiers on the platform barely paused. General Voor instructed a few soldiers to deal with the blaze, but that still left half a dozen more, including the one setting fire to the pyre where the prisoners stood. With the twitch of his hand, Auric created a heavy gust around the pyre which repeatedly put the fire out, while we continued forcing our way through the crowd. But the soldiers were relentless, and eventually they got a true blaze going.

We were still too far from the platform and I worried we'd be too late, but then Reven raised his hand and water suddenly began to fall from the sky over the prisoners. If I didn't know better I'd think rain was pouring down, even if it was isolated to one location.

As the pyre's flames were doused, the General scowled. "Curse this weather," he said, as he drew his sword. "We'll have to deal with these traitors another way."

As the other guards readied their weapons, Slade let out a low growl, and then the ground beneath the platform began to shake. I held onto his arm to remain steady, while people around us screamed and tried to flee from the sudden earthquake.

The soldiers and the prisoners both crumpled to their feet as the wooden platform broke apart with a huge crack and collapsed to the ground. The four of us rushed into the broken wood, trying not to injure ourselves on the splintered pieces. The prisoners were all still tied to their stakes and had landed at awkward angles, but a quick glance showed they were still alive.

Auric and I began freeing the prisoners, using our swords to cut through their bindings, while Slade and Reven guarded our backs as the soldiers got to their feet. The General tried to stand as well, but Auric knocked him back with a strong blast of air.

"Come with us!" I shouted to the prisoners, once they were free. I counted twelve of them total, some a little scorched and others bruised or cut, but alive. They stumbled after me off the ruined platform, looking dazed and scared, but at least they kept moving. Auric, Reven, and Slade formed a circle around us, fighting off the soldiers who tried to attack us.

The crowd had thinned between the fire and the earthquake, and those few people who were left didn't stop us as we pushed through them. I led the prisoners toward the shop Jasin had pointed out, hoping we were going in the right direction, especially since more soldiers were starting to rush after us.

I spotted Jasin on the corner of the street ahead of us and nearly cried out with relief that he was safe. He waved us forward and called out, "Hurry!"

Jasin led our ragged group into an alley in the back of the shops, where he shoved a large flower pot aside to reveal a metal grate in the ground. He yanked the grate open, and I gestured for the prisoners to go in first, while my other mates moved to fight off the approaching soldiers.

"Get inside, quickly!" Jasin said, as he helped the prisoners down into the hole. "Kira, you too."

I started toward him, but then I saw Reven cornered against the wall, fighting five soldiers at once, including General Voor. My assassin moved like a dancer, a swirl of black clothing and blades, but even with all of his deadly skill there were too many of them, and their armor was hard to penetrate. The General's sword slashed Reven's thigh, making him fall back against the wall, and terror gripped my throat.

I drew my sword and plunged it into the back of the soldier closest to me, desperate to save Reven before it was too late. I fought off the next soldier and threw myself in front of Reven before the General could run him through with his sword. My blade met the General's and I stared into his rage-filled eyes under that red winged helmet, before he knocked the sword from my hand with his massive strength.

Reven suddenly grabbed me and shoved me behind him, as he brought up his twin blades to fight General Voor again. He managed to force the man back, and then a huge rumble sounded above us. A gust of wind knocked me and Reven back, as part of the shop beside us split apart and crumbled, forming a wall of rubble between us and General Voor. Slade and Auric stood behind us, and had likely just saved our lives.

"Come on!" Jasin grabbed my arm and dragged me toward the tunnels, with the others right behind us. Auric helped Reven, who was limping, but then an arrow fired from somewhere and struck my prince in the shoulder, making him cry out. My heart twisted at the sound, but he didn't slow.

One by one we dropped into the tunnels, where the prisoners were waiting for us in the darkness. Slade was last, and once we were all safe he caused the ground to close up above us, preventing the soldiers from following—and trapping us inside.

30

SLADE

Jasin lit a torch, illuminating a lot of scared faces. "Is everyone all right?"

"I think so," the older woman said. Everyone hovered behind her, and I got the sense she was their leader.

Kira inspected the gash on Reven's leg with a frown, but he brushed her away. "I'm okay," he said.

She rested her hands on his thigh, near the wound, likely healing him as best she could. "You're not. We need to patch you up as soon as we get somewhere safe." She turned to Auric next to inspect the arrow in his shoulder.

"Thank you for saving us. My name is Daka." The older woman tilted her head as she watched us. "Are you part of the Resistance also?"

Kira hesitantly glanced at the four of us. "I suppose we are."

Daka nodded slowly. "The Gods must be on our side.

They helped us escape with the wind and the rain and that earthquake."

"Plus the cart on fire," Jasin added, with a grin.

"Yes, of course. We must not forget the Fire God for watching over us in our time of need."

The other prisoners nodded, and while they'd previously looked defeated, now hope shone in their eyes. None of them knew we had caused all of those things, which was a good sign that the soldiers didn't either. And I supposed in a way we were there on behalf of the Gods.

"But where will we go?" a man asked. He had his arm around a woman who leaned against him. "Nowhere in Ashbury will be safe for us now."

"We'll have to leave the city," the woman at his side said.

"There's a Resistance hideout about a day's ride north from here," I said. I never thought I'd get involved with the Resistance again, but it seemed my life was inevitably tied to them. "I can draw you a map."

Kira's eyebrows shot up and I knew she had questions for me, but they would have to wait. Auric pulled out his map and some paper from his journal, and while Jasin hovered over me with his torch for light, I sketched out what I remembered. What the woman I'd loved once had shown me on her own map, all those nights ago.

I handed Daka the map. "I hope this helps."

She examined it under the light. "Thank you. I think we'll be able to find this. We truly owe all of you our lives and so much more."

Jasin removed the fabric from around his mouth and

used it to wipe his face. "Come on. They'll find another way in to these tunnels soon, so we need to keep moving."

A young woman suddenly gasped and stepped back. "You. You're the soldier who killed my brother!" She pressed her back against the stone wall of the tunnel, her face pale. "He's one of them! The Onyx Army. He's going to turn us in!"

Kira stared at Jasin, who was grimacing, but then spoke quietly to the hysterical woman. "Yes, he was once part of the Onyx Army, but he's one of us now. I swear we're only trying to help you. And we need to get going."

"Come," Daka said, taking the other woman's hand. "What's past is past. Let's find our way to safety now so we have a future."

The younger woman stared at Jasin with terror in her eyes, but with some reluctance she nodded. Jasin's shoulders slumped when she finally turned away.

Our group walked slowly down the narrow tunnels after Jasin, who seemed to know where he was going. Reven's limp slowed him down, and when I moved to help him, I knew it must be pretty bad when he didn't protest my aid. Kira looked over with concerned eyes as the assassin leaned against me. She would be able to heal him, but we needed to make sure the soldiers didn't find us first.

When we reached the first junction, Jasin stopped to consider our location, before leading us down one of the diverging paths.

"Do you know where you're going?" Kira asked.

"Sort of," he said.

"More like getting us more and more lost," Reven muttered.

We walked for what seemed like hours, though it was hard to tell since there was nothing down here but the stone and the darkness. Others might feel claustrophobic in such a place, but not me. I would have been a good miner, but being a blacksmith had always felt like my true calling. Bending metal to my will was my strength even before I'd been given powers. Had I been shaped for this destiny my entire life, or was I chosen because of my affinity for metal and stone? I supposed I would have to ask the Earth God once I met him again.

Jasin stopped again, this time at a place where the tunnel diverged in three separate paths. He frowned, glancing around like he was looking for some clue. "I know it's not the left one, but I can't remember if the middle or the right leads outside the city."

Reven was right, Jasin was going to get us lost, and we didn't have time to waste. I rested my hand against one of the walls and closed my eyes. My senses expanded out and out, along the stone and rock, until a vague map of the tunnels formed in my mind. When I removed my hand and opened my eyes, I began walking down the middle path. "This way."

I guided us through the tunnels, brushing my fingers against the rough stone every now and then to make sure I was on the right path. As the walls grew closer and the air smelled fresher, I knew we were almost there.

At the last junction, I stopped and turned to the Resistance members. "If you follow this tunnel it will take you into the mountains where you should be able to get away."

"Thank you," Daka said, before turning to the rest of my companions. "Thank you all."

She shuffled down the tunnel and into the darkness, with the rest of the Resistance members following her. Once they were gone and I was sure they would make it out okay, I turned to the others. "Should we follow them?"

"We need to get back into the city and get our horses and supplies," Auric said, his voice weak. He was probably in a lot of pain from the arrow in his back.

"That might be dangerous," Jasin said. "Plus, we're on the opposite side of the city now."

"We need to stop somewhere soon," Kira said. "Both Reven and Auric need healing immediately or they won't be able to walk much longer."

"I'm fine," Reven muttered, but he was slumped against me and his face was pale.

Jasin ran a hand across his jaw as he considered. "There might be somewhere we can go near here."

"Somewhere safe?" Kira asked.

"Probably." He started back the way we came.

"Do you know how to get there from here?" I asked.

"Yeah, I know exactly where we are now."

"And where are we going?" Reven asked.

Jasin glanced at him. "Home."

31

KIRA

We emerged from the tunnels into what seemed to be the storeroom for a bakery. The air smelled of fresh bread and something sweet, making my stomach growl, but we didn't have time to delay. Reven and Auric were fading with every second, and while I'd done my best to stop their bleeding and take away the pain, I needed some quiet time with them in a safe place to heal them fully. Assuming I could, of course. My healing powers were still mostly untested and untrained. But I'd do whatever it took to keep them both alive.

As we walked out of the storeroom, the baker gave us a discreet nod, but didn't say a word. Was he with the Resistance too? I'd never thought much about their group when I lived in Stoneham and had always assumed they were somewhere far away, but maybe they'd been around me all along and I never knew it. Including Slade, it seemed. When we had a moment alone, I'd have to ask him how he'd known about the Resistance hideout.

We stepped out of the bakery and into the pouring rain, where night had fallen. As I pulled my hood over my head, Auric slipped and nearly fell, but Jasin caught him and helped him go on. Slade was already supporting most of Reven's weight at this point too. I wished I could do more than simply worrying about them. The streets were empty thanks to the downpour at least.

"Down here," Jasin said, as he turned down a street with a row of houses.

We stopped at the fourth house, which was done in the same sharp style as the others with a pointed roof and red trim. A pink flowering tree stood in front of it, the one cheerful thing in this entire miserable day. Was this Jasin's home? Was I about to meet his parents? Another thing to add to my list of worries.

Jasin paused at the front door as if hesitant, but then knocked on it. A beautiful woman in her forties with long, wavy auburn hair and Jasin's cheekbones opened the door and gasped. "Jasin! What are you doing here?"

"Can we come in?" he asked.

Her dark eyes swept over the rest of us and she opened the door wider. "Of course. Come inside and get dry."

We stepped into the house, which was warm and smelled faintly of a cozy fire. The furniture was dark and utilitarian with few trinkets, except for a sword hanging on one wall and a painting on the other. A chill ran through me when I got a closer look at the painting, which was beautiful even though it depicted the Black Dragon and her four mates sitting on top of a mountain, looking regal as they gazed out at the clouds with sunset hues behind them. It was both stunning to look at and terrifying to see it there.

"This is such a surprise," Jasin's mother said. "We thought you were stationed farther south."

"Jasin? I thought I heard your voice." A man with dark hair streaked with a touch of gray walked into the room. He paused when he saw the rest of us, no doubt an unexpected sight. Four strangers, completely soaked, and two of them injured. I didn't blame him for hesitating.

"Everyone, this is my mother, Ilya, and my father, Ozan. Mom, dad, these are...some friends of mine." Jasin glanced at the rest of us, before turning back to his parents with a grim face. "We're in a bit of trouble and need somewhere to lay low for the evening. Is it okay if we stay here?"

"What kind of trouble?" Ozan asked, his eyes narrowing.

Ilya waved him away. "Of course you can stay. Are you all in the Onyx Army with Jasin?"

"Not exactly," Slade said.

"I'll explain everything, but right now these two are injured and we need to treat their wounds," Jasin said.

"They can use Berin's bedroom," Ilya said.

She led us down a hallway with dark stone floors and opened the first door. We stepped inside a sparse room with a bed big enough for two people and little else. It looked like it hadn't been used in some time, but Ilya pulled out some blankets and pillows and got the bed ready for us.

"Thanks, Mom," Jasin said. "Let's leave them to it and I'll tell you what I've been up to."

With a nod to me and Slade, Jasin escorted his mother out of the room and shut the door behind them. Slade helped me ease Reven and Auric onto the bed, while they both groaned at the movement. It wasn't easy because they were both large, strong men, and their weapons and boots only made it harder.

Auric still had an arrow sticking out of his back, so he had to lie on his stomach. "Heal Reven first," he said, but his voice was weak.

"I'm fine," Reven said, his teeth gritted.

"Hold Auric down," I told Slade. "I'll get the arrow out."

Slade nodded and braced his weight on Auric's shoulders, keeping him in place. I wasn't sure what I was doing, although I'd removed arrows from lots of animals while hunting before, and this couldn't be all that different. I hoped.

I inhaled sharply, then pulled the arrow out with a quick, straight tug. Auric jerked and moaned and blood gushed from the wound. I rested my hand over it quickly to stop the bleeding, but his shirt was in the way. Although the bleeding slowed, I could sense that I needed more skin to skin contact if I was going to heal him fully.

"We need to get this off him," I told Slade, as I tugged at Auric's shirt.

Beside us, Reven had his eyes closed and I hoped he was okay, but I had to help Auric first. With much groaning from Auric, Slade helped me remove his cloak and shirt, along with his weapons, boots, and everything else except his trousers. But Reven was looking really pale too, and I worried he'd lost too much blood already.

"Reven too," I said, and Slade nodded.

We removed most of Reven's clothes as well, and had to slash open his trousers due to the gash on his thigh. I tried not to get distracted by all the muscular, naked flesh in front of me, and instead focused on what I could do to make them both better.

"Get in the bed with them," Slade suggested. "Your touch is what heals them."

Of course. I removed most of my own gear until I was in only my thin chemise, which was better since my clothes were soaked through with blood and water anyway. At first, I felt a touch of shyness at wearing so little around them, although they'd already seen me in my chemise over the last few nights. But then I pushed that feeling aside. These were my mates and they were all going to be seeing a lot of me soon, but more importantly, I didn't care how little I wore because all that mattered was healing Reven and Auric.

I crawled onto the bed between Reven and Auric, while Slade watched. His green eyes seemed to turn almost black as I slid between their bodies, and then he quickly looked away.

"I'll see about getting our horses," he said, his voice husky. He left the room before I could answer.

Was he jealous? Or aroused? I wasn't sure, but I couldn't think about that right now. Both Reven and Auric lay quietly with closed eyes and I couldn't tell if they were awake or not.

I took both of their hands first, working my fingers over their skin. Reven's hand was calloused, Auric's was smooth, and both of them dwarfed mine. I wasn't sure how to make my healing work, so I simply thought about how I wanted them to be healthy again. My feelings burned bright in my chest, surprising me with their intensity. I'd only known the men for a few days, but I already cared for them a great deal.

I wasn't sure if the healing was working and decided I needed to do more. I turned toward Reven, whose face was paler than normal. It was a miracle he'd been able to make it this far, although maybe my healing in the tunnels helped. I examined the wound and hesitated, then placed my hands on his thigh. The remains of his shredded black trousers hid the large bulge between his legs, but only barely. I tried not to stare at it, but my eyes kept finding their way back to that spot.

I pushed everything I felt into my touch as I ran my hands along his naked skin, feeling the hard muscles underneath my fingertips. After a few moments I began to see the wound close up. It was working!

He groaned and turned his head toward me, his eyes focusing on mine. He didn't say a word as I continued stroking his thigh, nor did he stop me when my other hand rested on his neck and moved up into his silky black hair.

"What are you doing to me?" he finally asked.

"Healing you." I trailed my fingers down his cheek and lightly touched his lips. Gods, he was beautiful. I so rarely got to be this close to him, or to stare into his eyes without him turning away. But for once he didn't move.

"Is that all?" he asked.

My breath caught. If I brought my lips to his and kissed him, would he stop me? Or would he kiss me back? If I shifted my hand slightly to brush against that bulge, would he pull away, or touch me in return?

Before I could gather my courage enough to try, he caught my hand in his and his eyes narrowed. "You protected me today and nearly got killed in the process. Don't ever do that again."

I yanked my hand away. "I couldn't let you die."

"I would have been fine. Just as I'm fine now." He rolled onto his side, facing away from me. "Don't trouble yourself further."

I stared at his back, wondering what that was about and trying not to feel rejected. But I didn't have the energy to worry about his behavior, not when Auric needed me too.

I turned to Auric next. His breathing was shallow and the arrow wound on his back—his very well-defined back— was deep. I rested my hands on his shoulder, sighing as our skin touched. As warmth spread from my fingertips, I slowly rubbed his shoulder and ran my hands down his back, spreading my healing to his entire body. Or that's what I told myself anyway. Maybe I just wanted to touch him some more.

His eyes fluttered open and he turned his head to smile at me. "Mm, that's nice."

I removed my hand and looked down at his shoulder,

which was now healed up as if it had never been injured at all. "How are you feeling?"

"Like a horse ran over me," he said, with a low chuckle.

"That sounds about right," Reven grumbled.

I settled myself between the two of them, their bodies pressed close against mine. "You both need rest and more healing, so we're going to lie here for a while, since skin to skin contact seems to be what works best."

"I'm not complaining," Auric said, as he rolled on his side and curled up against me. He kissed me, while one of my hands found his naked chest again, savoring the feel of his coiled muscle underneath his smooth skin.

Reven didn't say a word, but he turned onto his other side and stared at me with his dark, dangerous blue eyes. I was so tempted to kiss him, but I wasn't sure he wanted that from me. Instead I rested my hand on his strong chest too, and he reluctantly draped one arm around my waist.

With both men wrapped around me, I closed my eyes and felt a strange sort of contentment settle over me. The overwhelming desire for both of them was there too, but this was more than lust. This felt right, as if they both belonged by my side. The only way it could be better would be if Jasin and Slade were here too.

3 2

KIRA

After both Auric and Reven fell into a deep sleep, I slipped out of bed, donned my clothes again, and quietly left the bedroom. Voices drifted toward me from the front room, along with the smell of something delicious. I looked forward to getting to know Jasin's family, even if I wished it had been under better circumstances. Plus, I was curious about where he had grown up and excited about getting a glimpse into his past.

I stepped into the main room and the conversation died off as everyone turned to look at me. Jasin sat at a dining table made of shiny black stone with his parents across from him, though he jumped to his feet when he saw me. Slade was nowhere in sight, so he must still be getting the horses. I hoped he was safe.

Jasin moved to my side and took my hand to lead me to the table. "Mom, Dad, this is Kira. My...betrothed." He glanced at me with his eyebrows raised, as if asking if that was all right.

I smiled at him and inclined my head. Betrothed was probably the closest thing to the truth, since we couldn't exactly tell them what was really happening between us. "It's very nice to meet you both."

"Please join us," Ilya said. "We're about to have dinner and we're so happy you could be here with us."

"Thank you," I said.

Jasin pulled out a chair for me and I sat down, unable to keep a small smile off my face. These past few weeks had been difficult and at times unbelievable, and hours ago we'd been running for our lives, but this moment felt refreshingly normal. It was nice to pretend the only worry on my mind was getting his parents to like me. If I closed my eyes I could even imagine this was real, and that Jasin was my betrothed and soon we'd be married and settle down somewhere. Except that wasn't right, because I was missing the other men who shared my heart—but still, it was a nice fantasy to escape into for the time being.

Ilya began serving pasta with tomato sauce and tiny slivers of beef, a specialty of the Fire Realm that I hadn't eaten in years. A loaf of bread coated in garlic and butter was also passed around, and I felt bad that the others weren't there to share this feast with us. Hopefully there would be enough leftovers for the three of them.

I took a bite and it was the best thing I'd tasted in weeks. "This is delicious. I can see where Jasin gets his cooking skills from."

"Thank you," Ilya said. "Although I'm not sure I can take much credit for those."

"True, he's never made me anything this good," I said with a playful smile.

Jasin huffed. "Only because we've been traveling. A meal like this needs a proper kitchen and fresh ingredients and—"

I rested my hand over his. "I know, I was only teasing."

"Were you in the Onyx Army also?" Ozan asked in a blunt tone. Unlike Ilya, he didn't smile at us, but stared at me with dark, unwavering eyes.

"No, I wasn't," I said, glancing over at Jasin with uncertainty.

"Where did you two meet?" Ilya asked.

"I met her in a small village in the Earth Realm," Jasin said. "I showed up in her town and there was just this immediate connection between us."

He met my eyes with a grin and I smiled back at him as that connection he spoke of flared bright. It was true, even when I'd been scared of him or uncertain of our destiny, I'd always been drawn to him.

Ilya gave Ozan a knowing smile, but he continued to watch us with a surly expression. "Ozan and I were both in the army, stationed in Emberton," she said. "That's how we met. Of course, I retired from service when I had my boys, and Ozan took a permanent post in this city to stay close to us."

"Our entire family has always served in the Onyx

Army," Ozan said. "My father. His father." He looked pointedly at Jasin. "And my sons."

"I served for many years," Jasin muttered. "I did my duty."

"I can't believe you left," Ozan, his tone almost angry. "What were you thinking?"

"I was thinking that it was time for me to make a change," Jasin said. "The army wasn't for me, in the end."

"Not for you?" Ozan nearly yelled. "How can you say that after what happened to your brother?"

"Ozan..." Ilya said, resting a hand on his arm.

He shook it off and glared at Jasin. "And what about this trouble you're in now?"

"I already told you, I can't talk about that," Jasin said. He was normally so bold, but when facing his father, he'd shrunk back.

"Of course you can't. Don't tell me the army is after you?"

Jasin stared at his plate with his lips pressed into a thin line. When he didn't answer, that only made Ozan's face even angrier.

Ilya reached toward him again. "Ozan, please. Let's just enjoy our meal."

"No, I can't sit here and listen to this." Ozan shot to his feet. "One son dead and the other a deserter." He gave Jasin one last harsh look. "You bring shame to our family."

Without another word, he left the room.

Stunned silence descended over the table, until Ilya

said, "I'm sorry about that. He simply needs some time to calm down."

"It's our fault for showing up here unexpectedly," I said, glancing at Jasin, who stared down at his food with a pained expression. "We'll be gone first thing in the morning."

She waved a hand. "It's no trouble, really."

The front door open and I tensed, until I saw Slade's large figure filling up the doorway. He shut the door behind him and was drenched from the rain still pouring outside. "I moved the horses nearby and got our things."

"Thank you." I wanted to rush to him and give him a hug, so relieved to see him back safely, but I couldn't do that in front of Ilya without raising even more questions.

Slade joined us for the rest of the meal, although we spoke little after that. Jasin's normal vibrant self had dimmed thanks to his father's words, and I longed to get him alone so I could try to cheer him up.

When our meal was finished, I helped Ilya clean up in the kitchen, while Jasin and Slade spoke together in low voices about where he'd put the horses and the plan for tomorrow.

"I'm sorry again about my husband," Ilya said, as she set the plates aside. "Sometimes his temper gets the better of him. I wish our first dinner with you had gone better."

I nodded. "Can I ask what happened to your other son?"

"He was killed while fighting the Resistance outside Flamedale. It was supposed to be an easy raid, but it was a trap. His entire squad was slaughtered by those traitors." Her voice turned venomous, until she glanced over at her painting of the Dragons. "Thank the Gods that Sark came and took vengeance for us with his fire."

"I'm so sorry," I said, though my throat was tight. Jasin's family was completely loyal to the Black Dragon and supported her rule. No wonder Jasin had joined the Onyx Army when he was younger. How could he not, in this household? But if they found out what we truly were, I wasn't sure how they would react.

33

KIRA

While Slade slept in the front of the house, I checked on Reven and Auric, who were still passed out but seemed stable. Once I was sure they were fine, I joined Jasin in his old bedroom.

Like Berin's, this room was sparse, although it had more paintings done in the style of the one in the front room, plus a blank canvas in the corner. The first painting was of a man who looked a lot like Jasin swinging a sword while wearing the black scaled armor of the Onyx Army. The other painting was of the Crimson Dragon in flight, his wings spread while he blasted fire down at something below him.

"Did you do these?" I asked.

"I did, yeah," Jasin said, with some hesitation in his voice. Like he was worried what I would think about them.

"They're beautiful." I studied them closer, noticing the skill of the design and the blend of colors. I didn't know much about art, but I could tell Jasin was good, even if the subject matter was rather disturbing for me. "You're very talented."

He sat on the edge of the bed and began removing his boots. "Thanks. I once wanted to be an artist, but of course my parents didn't think that was a suitable career. My future was in the army and nothing else or they'd disown me."

"I got that feeling. It's a shame, because these are gorgeous." I tore my gaze from the dragon painting and examined the other one. "Is this your brother?"

"Yes. Berin was about my age there."

I took in the warrior's handsome, determined face. "You look like him."

"Do I? He was five years older than me and I always looked up to him. I thought he was perfect. My parents did too. When he died...it was a mess."

I turned back to Jasin. "Your mother said he died fighting the Resistance."

"He did, yeah." He looked away, his face pained. "And when I heard that, I volunteered to fight them too."

"That's how you knew about the tunnels."

"Actually, Berin and I found them when we were kids and used to play in them. But once I began hunting the Resistance, I realized their people were using the tunnels to hide and escape too. That's how I tracked them down. And I was damn good at it."

I swallowed, remembering the woman tonight who'd recognized Jasin. "The past is the past. Isn't that what you said?"

"Maybe, or maybe the past never leaves us," he said, his voice turning ragged. "You have no idea how many terrible things I've done. How many people I killed. Like that woman's brother. I don't remember her, but I probably did end his life."

I moved close to where he sat on the bed and placed my hands on his shoulders. "You're not that person anymore. Even before the Fire God came to you, you wanted to leave the Onyx Army."

His throat bobbed as he swallowed. "I couldn't stay. There was something I did that I couldn't forget. Something I'll never be able to forgive myself for."

"What happened?" I asked.

He didn't speak for some time, and when he did, he wouldn't meet my eyes. "General Voor found a town near the Air Realm border that he claimed was made up entirely of Resistance members. He sent my squad to kill them all. Men. Women. Children. Even their pets. Every living thing went up in flames. We didn't even need Sark for it." A shudder ran through his entire body. "I swore I would leave the army after that, but I was too much of a coward. I could only work up the nerve after the Fire God visited me."

I tilted his head up, forcing him to meet my eyes. "Maybe that's why he chose you. To give you this second chance."

He let out a bitter laugh. "Or maybe he chose me because I'm just like Sark."

"You're nothing like Sark." I pressed a kiss to his forehead. "Tonight you helped save those people from execution. Sark would never do that."

"I'm not sure that saving a few people tonight will ever make up for my past sins." He rested his head against my stomach and I gently stroked his hair.

"This was only the start of something bigger. And once we bond together, you'll be a much better Crimson Dragon than Sark ever was."

Jasin pulled back and gave me a smile with a hint of his usual flirtiness in it. "I'm looking forward to that."

"Being a dragon or bonding with me?"

"Both." His hands rested on my waist, his thumbs brushing against the fabric of my dress, and I felt a flicker of desire at his touch.

"Me too," I said, before bending down and finding his lips with mine. I kissed him softly, trying to show him I forgave his past and wanted a future with him, but it soon turned into more. Passion took over, making our kiss deeper, as if we couldn't get enough of each other.

We kissed with an almost desperate need as heat flared between our bodies. He dragged me onto his lap, making my dress bunch up around my waist as I straddled him. I gasped as his hard length pressed against my core, while his hands found my bare legs. His fingers smoothed along my skin ever so slowly, inching higher and higher, until they rested on my thighs, so close to where I ached for him.

Together we removed my dress and tossed it aside, leaving me in only my nearly see-through chemise. His large hands rested on my waist and our mouths found each other again, but then I tugged on his shirt, wanting it off. He lifted it over his head in one smooth motion, revealing that tanned, muscular chest I'd glimpsed before, not to mention his equally well-developed arms. I splayed my hands across his stomach, feeling the strength rippling beneath my fingertips, then began exploring up to his shoulders and down his arms. With each touch I wanted more of him.

I reached for his trousers but he caught my hand and stopped me.

"I'm ready," I told him.

"I'm not," he said.

I blinked at him. "You...don't want me?"

"Oh no, I do." He rolled his hips slightly, rubbing his hard length between my legs. "Trust me, I really do. But not tonight."

"I don't understand."

He stroked my face as he gazed into my eyes. "We should wait until we reach the Fire Temple."

"Why? I thought you wanted to get some practice in first."

"Not anymore." He pulled me down to the bed and drew the covers over us, then wrapped me in his arms. "When we bond together, I want you to know it's not just sex for me. With you, it's going to be a lot more."

I snuggled up against him. "I know, Jasin. I'm sorry I doubted you before, or worried about your past."

He touched my lips with his fingers. "You were right to doubt me. Before I met you, I was lost. I'd been told my life should be one thing, even though it never felt right. I let others mold me into what they wanted instead of standing up for what I believed in. I did things I wasn't proud of. I never let myself get attached to anything or anyone. But all of that changed once I was sent to find you. The Fire God might have given me these powers, but you gave me purpose. You gave me something to fight for. And I care about you more than you know."

My heart warmed from his words. "I care about you too, Jasin."

"Now sleep," Jasin said, pressing a kiss to my forehead. "Because once we reach the Fire Temple, I promise you won't be getting much sleep at all with all the naughty things I'll be doing to you."

"I like the sound of that." I shifted my leg so it draped over him, wanting our bodies pressed as close together as possible. Though I still burned with desire for him, it was just as good being held in his arms and knowing he cared for me the way I cared for him. Whatever doubts I'd once had about him were gone. I was ready for whatever we would face at the Fire Temple.

34

JASIN

"**G**et up!" someone whispered.

My eyes opened with a jolt. I was instantly alert, reaching for my sword and ready to fight. Someone moved in my bedroom, a dark figure in the meager light of dawn. I prepared to attack until I realized who it was. My mother.

I relaxed slightly, until I remembered Kira was in bed beside me wearing nothing but her little chemise. My mother knew we were sharing a room, and she definitely knew about my reputation with the ladies, but it was an entirely different thing to have your mother walk in on you in bed with a woman.

"Hurry," Mom said, before tossing my shirt in my face.

I threw it over my head. "What is it?"

Kira stirred beside me, but then let out a yelp and drew

the blanket up to cover herself when she saw who was in the room with us.

Mom peered through the curtains at the street outside. "Your father has done something terrible. You need to leave right away."

"Tell me." I grabbed my boots and began putting them on, while Kira quickly pulled on her dress.

Mom turned around with a frown. "He's gone to tell General Voor about you. They'll be here any minute now to arrest you as a deserter."

I swore under my breath as I jumped to my feet and strapped on my weapons. The sting of my father's betrayal cut deep, but I couldn't think about that yet. I had to focus. Remember my training. Get everyone out. Stay alive.

When Kira and I were dressed, we moved to the front of the house and found the others readying their things too. Everyone looked dazed and exhausted, but strong and alert. Slade was ready to go, and Auric and Reven both seemed to be completely healed, thanks to Kira's magic.

"It's best if you go out the back," Mom said, gesturing for us to follow her.

"How could he do this?" I finally asked, once we reached the back door.

"He's not thinking straight. I tried to talk some sense into him but he wouldn't listen." She shook her head. "I'm so sorry, Jasin."

I pulled my mother into a tight hug, while my heart hammered in my chest. When I pulled away, she turned to Kira to embrace her as well.

"I'm so happy I got to meet you," Mom said, before pressing a package into Kira's hands. "I wrapped up some food for all of you. Please take care of Jasin for me."

"I will," Kira said. "I promise."

We rushed through the door and out into the early morning light. Our horses were already waiting outside, tied to the fence with our things already packed on them. Slade had retrieved them last night and knew we might need to leave at a moment's notice.

I lifted Kira onto my horse, then climbed on behind her, securing my arm tight around her waist. For a second, I simply held her close, breathing her in while I tried not to think about how my father could turn me in as a deserter. Kira rested her hand over mine and gave it a squeeze.

"The north gate is nearby," I said, as I gathered my horse's reins.

"Let's go," Auric said.

We kicked our horses forward, but we didn't get far. At the end of the road, a row of mounted soldiers was already waiting for us. My father was in front of them—with General Voor at his side. The sight was like a dagger in my chest, though it didn't surprise me that he'd turned against me. I'd always been the disappointing son.

"There they are," my father said. "I knew they'd come this way."

"Halt," the General bellowed, sending a chill down my spine. How many times had I heard him shout out orders? How many times had he made me do things I'd later regret?

We were forced to stop and draw our weapons. My

sword was too large to wield while riding with Kira, but I pulled out my knife while my horse stomped his feet. Auric, Reven, and Slade also prepared to fight at our side.

"Get out of our way, and none of you will be hurt," I called out. "We don't want to fight you."

"Surrender, Jasin," Voor called out. "Turn yourself in and face the penalty for being a deserter, and we'll let your woman live."

A flash of anger made me see red and I nearly charged him for even mentioning Kira. "Never."

"You can't win this fight," General Voor said, shaking his great helmeted head.

"Want to bet?" Reven asked, his voice cold and deadly.

General Voor stared at Reven, before his gaze swept over the others. "You...you were there yesterday at the execution. You helped those Resistance traitors escape." He let out a harsh laugh. "Ozan, it seems your son is not only a deserter, but a traitor as well."

"Is this true?" my father asked me. "The Resistance killed your brother. How could you help them?"

With his confidence, passion, and anger, my father had always commanded my respect, along with my fear. General Voor was the same way. I'd admired them, followed them, and obeyed them. For years I went along with what they wanted because I thought I had no other choice, or I thought they knew better than I did. Now I realized I'd traded one overbearing, controlling, tyrant of a father for another. But I was no longer a coward, and I was no longer under their oppressive thumbs. Kira and the others had showed me that it was time to stand up for what I believed in.

I stared my father and General Voor down. "I left the army because I could no longer follow orders when I knew they were wrong. And I helped those people because it was the right thing to do."

"You really are a traitor," my father said, then spat on the ground. "May Sark's flames turn your bones to ash."

"Get them," General Voor said.

At his command the soldiers charged toward us on their horses. Rage burned hot inside me, and I no longer cared if anyone knew about my magic. If my father wanted flames, I'd show him some damn flames.

I spread my hand and fire leaped up from the ground in front of us, creating a blazing wall between us and the soldiers. Once it was as high as my house, I yanked on the reins to turn my horse around. "This way!"

While the soldiers shouted and fell back from the flames, I led the others down the empty early morning streets toward the north gate. There would be soldiers there too, but it was the closest escape and we had to get out of this city fast.

Our horses galloped through the stone streets toward our destination. I gripped Kira tightly as I led the charge, praying I remembered the quickest route. Her other mates rode right at our heels.

Just when I thought we'd gotten away, General Voor appeared before us with two other soldiers. Slade flicked his hand and a stone wall crumpled down on top of the soldiers, sending them to the ground. I gave him a short nod as we continued racing through the streets.

I spotted the heavy stone gate up ahead and was relieved to see it was already open. Merchants and other travelers were already moving through it with their carts, forcing us to slow as we maneuvered around them.

"Stop them!" a soldier called out behind us.

The guards at the gate jumped to attention, grabbing their swords and bows. Two of them charged at us, but Auric blasted them both back against the wall. With a shout, we urged our horses forward and made it through the gate, but we weren't safe yet—not from the archers on top of the wall, who prepared to fire at us.

"I've got this," Reven said.

As the arrows flew, he pulled all the water out of the moat and sent it flying straight up, where it froze mid-air and formed a tall wall of ice between the archers and us. Impressive.

"Into the mountains!" I called out.

Our horses clambered up the rough, rocky slope, where the trees and brush soon blocked view of us, though I had no doubt the soldiers would be chasing after us soon. I kept looking behind us, expecting to see the General or my father, but the way behind us remained clear.

We pushed our horses hard until the sun was high in the sky, and Kira held my hand the entire time. Although it burned me up inside knowing my father had betrayed me and that I would never be able to go home again, it was all worth it—for her.

35

KIRA

After a long, exhausting day of riding up and down mountains on the way to the volcano, Slade found us a cave to hide in for the night. We'd seen no sign of the Onyx Army behind us so far, but that didn't mean they weren't following. Our only hope was to get to the Fire Temple and hope we would be safe there—or that we'd unlock Jasin's dragon form and be able to blast our way out.

We ate the leftover pasta Ilya had packed for us, but instead of sitting around a campfire and chatting, all the men retreated to different corners of the cave or slipped outside to be alone with their thoughts. I was surprised to find that I wanted the opposite of solitude and missed their company. After nearly two weeks with these men, I'd started to grow accustomed to having them by my side at all times.

"Can I sit here?" I asked Slade, who was sharpening his axe.

"Of course." He set down his axe and patted the spot on the blanket beside him.

I sank down beside him with a weary sigh. "Thanks. It's been a long day."

"Been a long week."

"True. But between fighting off soldiers, helping prisoners escape, and running up and down mountains, I'm feeling especially weary." I leaned back on my hands, stretching my legs out. "Do you think the Resistance members got away safely?"

"I hope so. Our escape this morning might have helped distract the soldiers who would have followed them."

I hadn't thought of that, but I nodded. "How did you know about that Resistance hideout?"

He ran a hand along his dark beard. "I used to be part of the Resistance."

"You were?" I blinked at him. "Did you fight against the Onyx Army with them?"

"No, nothing like that. I made weapons and hid some of them when they were in trouble. That was all."

"How did you get involved with them?"

"A friend convinced me to help them, but I tried to keep my involvement as minimal as possible. I didn't want to bring trouble to my town or to my family and friends." He frowned as he glanced at his axe. "Trouble found me anyway though."

"I know what you mean," I said with a sigh. "At some point we might want to find the Resistance and convince them to help us. It could be good to have some allies."

"We can try, although the Resistance survives by staying hidden. They might not be interested in helping us."

I thought of my parents, wondering again if they were also members of the Resistance, or if they were truly killed because of me. Or both.

"I suppose we'll worry about that later." I rested my hand on his arm. "But thank you for everything you did in Ashbury."

"It was nothing." He met my eyes and something stirred inside me as I admired his rugged, handsome face. I wanted to run my fingers through that beard and see if it was as soft as it looked. I wanted to kiss those sensual dark lips. As he looked back at me, I thought I sensed a similar desire smoldering inside him, but then he turned away and went back to sharpening his axe.

Sensing that our moment was over, I got up and walked over to Auric, who was studying a map he'd laid flat on a wide rock.

"How are you feeling?" I asked him. "Any problems with your shoulder?"

"None." He stretched his back and arms. "If I didn't know better, I'd think I'd never been injured."

"Good." I leaned against his side and peered at the map. "How close are we?"

"I think we're about here," he said, pointing to a spot in the mountain range cutting through the Fire Realm. He traced his finger across to a large black peak. "The Fire God's temple is here, near the Valefire volcano, on the edge of the Eastern Sea. I estimate we should reach it by tomorrow afternoon."

I nodded and wrapped my arms around myself. A confusing mix of emotions swirled inside me at the thought of reaching the end of this journey tomorrow. I was torn between feeling nervous, anxious, excited, and worried. I had no idea what to expect at the Temple, and I wasn't sure I was ready for what we would face there.

Auric must have sensed my unease, because he gave me a warm smile. "Don't worry. There should be priests at the Temple to guide you through what you need to do. Hope-fully they can give us more information too."

"That would be good," I said, although I wasn't very enthusiastic.

"Are you hesitant about sleeping with Jasin?"

"A little." I glanced over at Jasin, who sat alone, staring into the fire he'd made. "Not because I don't want to do it. But it's my first time, and there's a lot of pressure riding on this."

"I understand." He took my hands in his. "For what it's worth, I think Jasin will take good care of you."

"Does it bother you, knowing you have to share me with him?"

"No, but it's common for people in the Air Realm to have multiple partners." He shrugged. "Obviously I would have liked to be first, and Jasin wouldn't be my choice to share you with, but he's loyal. Whatever he might have done in his past, he cares about you a lot. Everyone can see it."

"Thanks. I should probably go talk to him."

"Yes, you should." He gave me a quick kiss, then released my hands and went back to studying his map.

I joined Jasin by the fire and sat beside him, trying not to let my fear of the flames show. "I'm so sorry about what happened this morning."

He nodded, his face solemn. "I never thought my father would do something like that. I can only hope that one day my parents will forgive me and understand why I chose this path. Seems unlikely though."

I leaned against him, resting my head on his shoulder. "You did what you thought was best. I'm proud of you, even if they're not."

He pressed a kiss to the top of my head. "That's all I need to hear."

We sat in companionable silence as the flames crackled and popped in front of us, until I said, "Auric told me we'll reach the temple tomorrow."

"Good. I'm ready." He pulled back to look into my eyes. "Are you?"

"I think so. I'm still nervous about a lot of things, but I want to do this."

He arched an eyebrow. "Nervous about being with me?"

"Yes, and about all the fire." I swallowed. "I couldn't handle that burning house. What am I going to do in the Fire Temple? Or once you're a Dragon or I have fire magic of my own?"

He wrapped an arm around me. "I won't let any harm come to you, I promise. And once you have this magic, I'll train you. Reven would never admit it, but I've gotten a lot better over the last few days thanks to our training."

"Yes, you have. I was suitably impressed by the wall of flame earlier."

His cocky smile returned, and some of the melancholy lifted from his eyes. "Were you scared?"

"No, I wasn't," I said, surprised by my answer.

He let out a long breath. "I know you haven't always trusted me—both with my fire and with your heart, so that means a lot to me."

"I do trust you," I said, and meant it. Although his past reputation with women had worried me at first, I sensed his passion for me more than from any of the other men. Jasin wasn't the type to hold back—he said what he felt, often without thinking first, and that was one of the things I loved about him. You never had to worry about where you stood with him.

He brushed his lips against mine. "I'm ready for tomorrow. I want to be yours, and I want you to be mine."

"Me too."

He pulled me close and kissed me with all that pent-up passion, until I had to pull away to stop from dragging him down to the blanket to continue what we started last night, even with the other guys watching. Although I wouldn't mind if the guys watched, actually. Or joined in. I glanced over at Auric and Slade at that thought, but they were both pointedly not looking at us, as if trying to give us some privacy. But the fourth member of our group was nowhere to be seen.

"Where's Reven?" I asked, as I pulled away from Jasin.

Jasin shrugged. "Outside maybe?"

I sighed. "I should go check on him."

I slipped through the low entrance of the cave and into the small valley outside. Under the tiny sliver of a moon, Reven stood beside his horse, unpacking something from one of his bags. No, not unpacking—he was putting something in them.

"What are you doing?" I asked.

He turned his black-haired head toward me. "I'm leaving."

My stomach fell out from under me so fast I was nearly dizzy. "What? Why?"

"I never planned to be part of this team. Last night reminded me of that."

"Last night you helped those people. You saved my life. And after that..." I took a step toward him. "I started to think you cared about me. About our mission. What changed?"

"What changed is that you risked your life for me."

"I don't understand...why is that bad?"

"You nearly got yourself killed in the process. And today General Voor recognized me because of it, putting the entire group at risk." He shook his head, his voice dripping with disgust. "Caring for people makes you weak. I should have left a long time ago."

My throat tightened and I found it hard to speak. He was really leaving, just when I'd thought he was starting to truly be part of the group—and had started to have feelings for me. "What about the Water God?"

He shrugged as he closed up his pack. "He can find someone else to be his Dragon. Maybe he'll let you choose someone better this time."

The thought of having anyone else as the Azure Dragon and the fourth member of my team was too horrible to even consider. My entire soul rejected the very idea. "What if I choose you?"

He gave me a sharp glance. "That isn't an option."

"But we need you." I stepped closer, placing a hand on his chest. "I need you."

He gazed into my eyes and I saw a hint of something like desire there, which made me think he might stay after all. That all of this was just his way of trying to protect his heart and he didn't mean any of it, not really. When he took my hand my hope grew, but all he did was drop it.

"You'll have to find someone who gives a damn," he growled. "I have no desire to be an enemy of the Onyx Army. I get a lot of business from them."

I stumbled back, shocked and hurt by his words. "Is that all you care about? Business?"

"I care about surviving. And I need to look out for myself and no one else. You should do the same."

"But you know what we're fighting for. How can you walk away?" I wanted to shout and cry and beg him to stay. "Whose side are you even on?"

He pulled the hood over his head. "I'm on no one's side but my own. Thought you'd realized that by now."

"Reven, this isn't you. You're a good man. I know you are."

"That's where you're wrong." He swung up onto his black horse and look down at me. "You keep trying to make me into a hero, but you need to get this through your pretty head: there are no heroes in this world, and if there were, I wouldn't be one of them."

"Then go," I said, practically shaking with anger and disbelief. "If that's how you feel, then I don't want you here anyway."

"Trust me, you're better off without me."

And with that, he rode into the darkness, while I stared after him too shocked and heartbroken to even say goodbye.

36

AURIC

I folded up the map and put it away, then pulled out my journal to record my daily log of our journey. The others thought it was a waste of time, but someday my notes might be useful to someone else, perhaps the next people to follow in our footsteps.

I moved closer to the fire for more light, where Jasin was staring into it with a brooding expression. He wasn't normally a brooder—that was more Reven's style—but he had good reason after today's events.

I debated a moment before sitting near him. Jasin and I didn't get along on the best of days, but I wanted to change that. "Jasin, I'm sorry about what happened with your parents."

He inclined his head slightly. "Thanks."

"For what it's worth, I know what it's like to be the youngest brother and the disappointing son."

"Oh yeah?" He chuckled softly. "I bet your father would never betray you like that though."

"I'm not sure. I suppose we'll find out once we reach the Air Realm." Unease settled over me as I considered our next step after the Fire Temple. "I doubt I can hide from them once I return. Either way, it's a shame you had to experience such a thing."

Before he could respond, Kira burst into the cave, her face flushed and her eyes watering. Each one of us jumped to our feet.

"Are you all right?" Slade asked.

"Reven's gone," she said.

"What do you mean, gone?" Jasin asked.

She wrapped her arms around herself. "He left. He doesn't want to be one of my mates."

The others looked as shocked as I felt. Leave Kira? That was impossible. Even though we hadn't officially bonded yet, I couldn't imagine being anywhere except by her side, supporting her however I could. How could Reven not feel the same?

I took her into my arms and held her close. "I'm sorry."

As she rested her head on my shoulder, Jasin joined us and embraced her from behind. "He's an idiot," he said.

"I knew he wanted to leave, but I never thought he'd actually do it," Slade said. He remained back, but looked hesitant, as if he wanted to join but wasn't sure he should.

Kira pulled back and wiped at her damp eyes. "What do we do now?"

"The only thing we can do," I said. "Keep going."

37

KIRA

I glanced behind us for the hundredth time, hoping to see Reven's dark profile or his black horse, but he was never there.

"He's not coming back," Auric said. "I'm sorry, Kira."

With a sigh, I tightened my arms around Auric and rested my head on his shoulder. "Maybe, but it's hard to accept he's truly gone."

He guided the horse around a large boulder. "I know. But now you can find someone who really wants to be here."

I tried to think of it that way, but I couldn't shake the feeling that Reven's departure had left a huge hole in my heart. I'd thought we'd begun to develop something real, but clearly, I was wrong. Even though he'd kept his distance from me, I'd still felt the same connection with him that I did the other men. At first, we could pretend it was simply the magic drawing us together, but not anymore. The fact that Reven could leave proved there was no magic forcing him or the other men to stay with me.

As we approached Valefire, the volcano where the Fire Temple was located, the landscape became stark and ominous. The dense shrubs and scraggly trees began to thin out and the land became black from lava that had once spilled. Steam and boiling water kept bursting from holes in the ground, and we had to go around numerous deep craters the closer we got to the slope of the volcano.

I'd expected Valefire to look like a tall mountain, but instead it was more of a mound with a flat top, where a large plume of white smoke billowed into the bright blue sky. The ocean could be spotted behind it, along with more thick smoke.

Jasin stopped his horse suddenly, staring at the sky. "The volcano...it's erupting."

"That can't be right," Auric said. "The volcano is supposed to be dormant."

"It was. People used to walk right up to the crater and drop offerings in for the Fire God."

"Are we in any danger?" I asked.

"I doubt the Fire God would try to stop us now," Slade said.

Auric peered at the volcano. "We should be safe, since it doesn't appear to be too violent of an eruption."

"Where is the Temple?" I asked.

"It's at the top," Jasin said, his face grim.

I nodded. "Then we keep going."

The terrain became even rougher as we reached the

base of the volcano. There was nothing living in sight, not even a weed. The blackened ground had strange rope-like patterns in it, which I realized were from a previous eruption where the flow of lava had hardened and solidified. The volcano rose high above us, under its swirling cloud of white smoke.

With great reluctance, we left our horses behind and took only what we needed for the climb. The slope up was full of black volcanic formations, mounds, and ridges, and we stumbled up it. More steam shot out in various places from vents in the earth, and the air grew heavy with heat and a smell like rotten eggs. I coughed and covered my mouth and nose with a cloth, while my eyes began to burn and sweat dripped down my forehead.

The climb was brutal, and at times I thought I might give up, but I kept going with encouragement from my three mates. We stopped for short water breaks and nothing more, even when our muscles began to ache and the sun slowly set behind us. *Only a few more steps*, I told myself over and over, until we finally reached the summit.

The ground was flat and smooth, before dropping suddenly into a crater in the center. An eerie orange glow rose up from the crater, illuminating an impressive building made of black glassy stone with tall, pointed towers.

A beautiful woman I guessed to be in her forties stood in front, wearing a red silk robe with black trim. She had pale blond hair and bowed low when we approached. "Greetings, ascendants."

I glanced at the others warily. "Were you expecting us?"

"Yes. Ever since Valefire erupted a little over a month ago, we knew the Fire God was stirring and new Dragons were rising." She swept her gaze across the men. "Which one of you has been chosen by the Fire God?"

"I was," Jasin said, stepping forward.

"Show me his gift."

Jasin spread his palm and summoned a ball of fire in the middle of it. The woman smiled and watched the flames flicker, then produced a matching one in her hand, making us gasp.

"How...?" he asked.

"My name is Calla, and I am the High Priestess of the Fire God." She closed her hand and the flame vanished. "Like you, I've been gifted a touch of his power in order to serve him."

"Does that mean you're a Dragon also?" Auric asked.

"No, that is your destiny and not mine." She frowned as she glanced between us again. "I expected four men, though."

My throat clenched up at the reminder. "One of them didn't want to be here."

"No matter. You only need the Crimson Dragon's ascendant today." She gestured toward the tall door of the temple, her long sleeves flowing around her. "Please come inside."

We followed her into a huge entry room with a large domed ceiling and dozens of torches, which seemed to flare brighter as we approached. I tried to ignore the flicker of fear inside me at the sight and kept walking toward a tall dragon statue made of the same smooth black stone as the rest of the

Temple. Four older, handsome male priests waited for us in front of it, wearing similar robes to Calla's. They all bowed low as we drew near.

"These are the Fire God's priests," Calla said, as she smiled at the four men. "And my mates."

I'd heard that the High Priestesses followed the ways of the Spirit Goddess and the Black Dragon and took four mates in the same tradition, but I was never sure if it was true or simply rumors. Perhaps she'd be able to give me advice on managing four men with strong personalities.

We all exchanged names, while the priests stared at me and Jasin with both awe and curiosity.

"It is an honor to meet you," Blane, the first priest said.

"We've been waiting for you for a very long time," another priest named Derel said.

"You were?" I asked. "How?"

"It's time you learned the truth about the Dragons," Calla said. "But first, you're probably in need of some refreshments."

She led us into another large room with a long black table that was already prepared for a feast. Our exhaustion took over as we sank into the stone chairs, and two of the priests began pouring us red wine and cool water, while the others served us glazed beef with vegetables and pasta shells. I eagerly downed an entire glass of water before diving into my meal.

"What can you tell us about the Dragons?" I asked, once my weariness began to fade thanks to their delicious food.

Calla was sitting across from me and took a sip of wine.

"The Black Dragon and her mates have ruled the world for the last six hundred and thirty years—but it was not always that way."

Auric leaned forward, hungry for her knowledge. "What do you mean?"

"Thousands of years ago, the Gods created elementals and humans. They believed we could exist in harmony. They were wrong. When humans began expanding into elemental lands the elementals fought back and we were no match for their magic. The Gods created the five Dragons to be their representatives, blessing those chosen humans with the powers of the elementals in order to protect the world and keep the balance. The Dragons acted as intermediaries between the two groups, and for many years there was peace."

Jasin paused between bites. "I thought the Dragons were supposed to rule us."

"Not originally," Blane said, as he refilled my water. "They were peacekeepers and protectors, not rulers. Instead, each Realm governed itself. Until Nysa."

"The Black Dragon," Slade said quietly, while a shiver ran down my spine at her name.

"What changed with her?" Auric asked.

Calla folded her hands in front of her. "Before Nysa, a new set of Dragons was chosen every fifty years. That way, none of the Dragons could gain too much power. But Nysa found a way to become immortal and stop new Dragons from being chosen."

"How?" Slade asked.

"No one knows. At first, the priests thought the Gods had gifted her with a longer reign because they were pleased with her work. But then the Gods stopped speaking to their priests and seemed to vanish from the world completely. Some believed they'd forsaken us or passed control to the Dragons. Others thought they were sleeping or dead. But I was visited by the Fire God twenty years ago, and he told me to prepare for your arrival. He began stirring again forty days ago."

"That was my birthday," I said. "When all of this began."

She nodded. "New Dragons were always chosen on the Black Dragon's twentieth birthday. For whatever reason, the Gods have woken again and they have selected all of you."

Jasin nodded slowly. "The Fire God came to me and told me to find Kira and bring her to this temple. Now what?"

Calla gave us both a knowing smile. "You and Kira must go into the altar room and bond, while the others wait here. Are you ready to begin?"

"I suppose so," I said, suddenly nervous as I glanced over at Auric and Slade.

"Your other mates will be well attended to, so you do not need to worry," Derel said.

"Thank you," Auric said. "I'm wondering if you have any old texts about the Gods or the Dragons I could look at."

"Certainly," Blane replied.

I rose to my feet and my three mates immediately stood

in response. I glanced over at Jasin, my heart pounding. It was time.

Auric wrapped his arms around me, before turning to Jasin and giving him a nod. "Good luck."

"Treat her well," Slade grumbled at Jasin, before giving me a short nod. The four priests led them into another room, leaving me and Jasin alone with Calla.

"Follow me," Calla said, as she led us out of the dining hall and back to the main room. She took us to a tall black door with two dragons carved into it. "No one has used this room for about six hundred years, but we've prepared everything for you." She stopped in front of it and smiled at both of us. "Take as much time as you need. Once you've bonded, go through the other door."

Jasin reached out and took my hand. I held it tight and swallowed the lump in my throat as the door opened for us.

38

REVEN

My horse moved slowly over the rocky, hostile terrain while my thoughts churned. I'd followed behind the others at a distance to make sure they made it to the Fire Temple unharmed, but now my duty was over. I could leave.

I *should* leave.

So why didn't I?

I would love to blame it on magic, but I'd ridden far enough away last night to confirm there was nothing forcing me to be with Kira. The Gods had made me find her, but that was all. There was nothing tying us together now.

I drew in a long breath and turned my horse away from the volcano, urging her west. Kira didn't need me anymore. She was no doubt inside the Fire Temple already getting nice and cozy with Jasin. Once she was done, she could find another man to be her Azure Dragon.

It couldn't be me. The incident in Ashbury had made that all too clear.

If I closed my eyes I could still clearly picture Kira throwing herself in front of me, trying to protect me from those soldiers, and nearly getting herself killed in the process. A sharp spike of panic had struck me then, as it did now at the thought of her dying because of me. Like the last woman I'd loved.

Mara had been killed because of me, and I swore I'd never let that happen again. Years ago, I'd been unable to save her, and now I'd nearly failed Kira too. Which is why I had to leave. Caring for someone made you weak and only put them in danger. The sooner Kira stopped caring for me, the better.

My brooding thoughts were disturbed when I spotted some dark figures riding toward the volcano. Soldiers. They must have tracked us here from Ashbury.

Not my problem, I told myself. *Not my fight.*

I urged my horse forward, planning to keep my distance from the armored men. Kira and her remaining mates would be able to fight them off, especially once Jasin became a Dragon. They didn't need me. And I certainly didn't need or want them.

So why did I feel like I was making the biggest mistake of my life?

Jasin and I stepped into another domed room made of that same black stone, with torches lit around a raised platform. In the center of it was a large bed decorated with red and black silk sheets and lots of soft-looking pillows. If I had any doubt before about what we were meant to do, it vanished now.

I ran my hand along the smooth wall as I slowly made my way toward the platform. "This stone is beautiful."

Jasin climbed the steps to the bed without hesitation and began removing his weapons and armor. "It's obsidian. Volcanic glass. Lots of jewelry in the Fire Realm is made from it. I've never seen an entire building though."

I followed him onto the altar and wrung my hands, feeling awkward. "Now what?"

He raised an eyebrow. "Do I need to explain to you how this works?"

"No," I said, my cheeks flushing. "It's just all so...forced."

A frown crossed his mouth. "If you don't want to do this..."

"I do," I said quickly, taking his hands. "Sorry, forced was the wrong word. It's just hard to get in the mood knowing seven people are out there waiting for us to get on with it. And what will happen once we do? Reven left. Fire still scares me. The Onyx Army is following us." I shook my head. "I don't feel ready to become the Black Dragon. Maybe I never will."

He drew me into his arms. "Do you doubt me?"

"No." I let out a nervous laugh. "This situation is just not very romantic."

"Maybe I can help with that."

He took my chin and captured my mouth in a smoldering kiss. Passion ignited instantly at his touch, as if it had been building inside me and could now finally be freed. As he kissed me harder, I wrapped my arms around him, desperate for more.

His mouth trailed down my neck, sending delicious tingles through my body. "Forget about everyone else. Tonight is about you and me. And I've been wanting to do this for a very long time."

"You have?" I asked, breathless.

"Since the first time I fell on top of you in the woods." His lips brushed against my collarbone. "Don't tell me you didn't feel the spark between us too."

"I did. I do."

He stepped back and reached down to grip the edge of his shirt, his eyes never leaving mine. As he lifted the fabric up, I let my gaze fall to his chest, watching the way his muscles rippled with the movement. He tossed the shirt aside, before his hands moved to the front of his trousers. He paused and one of his eyebrows arched, as if he was waiting for me to stop him. When I didn't move, he eased them off and kicked them aside, making me suck in a breath.

He wore nothing underneath.

"Like what you see?" he asked, with that cocky grin I loved.

I could only nod and stare, my throat dry. I'd seen a naked man or two before, and had nearly slept with one once, but Jasin was truly blessed by the Gods in every way. I took him all in, my eyes following the V of his hips to the large cock jutting from between his muscular thighs. Maybe *I* was the one who was blessed.

Hoping to show him I was just as eager for this as he was, I removed my dress, leaving me in only my chemise. He'd seen me in it before, but his eyes tracked my movements with hunger anyway. I slowly lifted the chemise over my head, making me as naked as he was.

"Gods, you're beautiful," Jasin said. "I could look at you for hours."

"Are you only going to look?" I asked, with a teasing smile.

"Oh no. I'm going to do a lot more than that." He set his hands on my hips, his fingers warm on my bare skin. "I'm going to touch. I'm going to taste. And then I'm going to make you mine."

He took me in his strong arms and lifted me up, then smoothly put me down on the bed with him on top of me. Our bodies were lined up, skin to skin, and I felt his hard shaft nudge between my thighs. A rush of need made me arch up against him, my breath quickening.

"I'm ready," I said, as I looked up at his handsome face.

He chuckled softly as he nuzzled my neck. "Oh, now you're impatient?" His lips danced across my skin like a tease. "We're just getting started."

His mouth moved down until he found my breasts, where my nipples were already hard for him. A soft moan escaped me as his tongue lazily slid over one taut bud, while his fingertips circled the other. When he sucked that nipple into his mouth, it sent heat straight to my core. My head fell back and my fingers tangled in his thick hair as he took his time with each breast, slowly driving me mad for him.

"Jasin," I gasped. "Please."

I wasn't sure what I was begging for, but Jasin moved lower at my words. His lips traced the underside of my breasts, trailed down my stomach, and brushed along my hips. With each touch my desire flared higher and higher, until my entire body clenched with need. Only then did he spread my legs wide and dip his head between my thighs.

At the first touch of his mouth, I gasped and nearly jolted off the bed. His hands gripped my hips, holding me steady as his tongue slowly swept along my folds. Pleasure simmered inside me with his warm breath on my skin, his rough stubble between my thighs, and his fingers moving to my bottom, lifting me up to his lips like an offering.

When his mouth found my most sensitive spot, I grasped the sheets and cried out. When one of his fingers slipped inside me, I thought I might surely die. It was too much, and yet I didn't want him to stop. He was the one worshipping me, but I was the one whimpering and begging for release. When he slid a second finger into me, my climax burst like a bonfire on a dark night, and I could do nothing but succumb to it.

As my body trembled, Jasin slowly moved up it, covering my skin with his own. "*Now* you're ready."

He nudged my thighs wider and moved between them, then took himself in hand and slowly rubbed between my folds, getting nice and slick. I was nearly dizzy with anticipation and almost started begging him again, when he guided himself inside.

Gods, he was big. And delightfully warm too, like sinking into a hot bath after a long, hard day. I felt every inch as he pushed deeper, and he watched my face the entire time, checking if I was in any pain. But nothing hurt, except this burning need within me that needed to be sated.

"More," I managed to say.

He gave me a self-satisfied smirk, then buried himself in me with one easy thrust. I cried out, not in pain, but from the sudden pleasure from being stretched and filled so completely. Our eyes met and the connection between us, the one I'd felt ever since we'd first met, burned hotter.

Jasin kept his eyes on mine as he began moving inside

me with slow, smooth strokes. At first the pressure was intense and almost uncomfortable as my body adjusted to his size, but then it quickly gave way to the most amazing sensations. My hips began to buck in time to his thrusts as the delicious tension grew between my legs.

As if sensing my need, he pinned me down and took my mouth, while my hands found the hard planes of his back. He rocked deep inside me, our bodies moving together in a smooth rhythm that made my heart nearly burst because everything about this moment was so *right*. I was meant to be with Jasin, just as he was meant to be with me. And soon I'd be sharing this moment with my other men too.

But then Jasin sat back on his heels and dragged my hips up, making my back arch as he moved deeper inside me, hitting me at an angle that made me see stars. He reached a hand between us and began rubbing me at the same time. With each thrust he stroked the flame higher and higher until I thought I would truly combust.

"Come for me, Kira. Show me you're mine."

With his other hand on my bottom to guide my hips, Jasin coaxed an explosive orgasm out of me that had me moaning and writhing underneath him like some kind of wild beast. I clenched around him, squeezing him tight as he pounded me faster and gave himself over to the pleasure too.

Flames suddenly burst over Jasin's skin and I cried out at the sight, but we were both too far gone to do anything to stop it. He groaned and bent over me, pressing our bodies close as we both found our release together. His mouth claimed mine while the fire engulfed us, so bright it lit up the entire chamber. But it didn't burn my skin.

Intense flame roared through me, so strong I lost all trace of myself, and simply became fire and light and heat. But then came an overwhelming sense of Jasin, as if we were truly one, like two halves of a whole that had finally been put back together after far too long. I *knew* him, just as he knew me. And he was *mine*.

When I came back to myself, Jasin held me in his arms, while the last shudders of pleasure faded from our bodies. The fire was gone, as if it had never been there at all.

"What was that?" I asked.

Jasin pressed a soft kiss to my lips. "I think we're bonded now."

40

SLADE

I stared at the stark black stone walls, as if admiring the architecture of the temple could actually distract me from my thoughts. Auric leaned over a book and chatted with one of the priests about it like it was the most fascinating thing in the world. I supposed that was his way of dealing with the fact that Kira was on the other side of that wall sleeping with Jasin right now.

I crossed my arms. Why did it bother me so much? It's not like I wanted to be in there with her instead. Okay, maybe I did, but I *shouldn't* want that. Auric and Jasin were both in love with her, that was obvious. Reven was gone, after fleeing in the night like a villain. And then there was me. I cared for Kira a lot, but I wasn't sure I could ever give her my heart completely. Or get used to the idea of sharing her with three other men.

I'd heard that taking multiple partners was common in

the Air and Water Realms, but after what I'd been through with Faya, the thought made my chest ache. This would be different, of course—Kira's mates were open about all of us sharing her, and it was part of our divine duty—but I worried it would still lead to heartbreak and trouble.

Even so, I would never leave like Reven. I would stay and do my duty, to fulfill the destiny the Gods had bestowed upon me, and to protect Kira however I could. I'd just have to protect my heart at the same time somehow.

The sound of footsteps and a door slamming caught all of our attention. Auric slammed the book shut and gave me a wary glance. I grabbed my axe, then led the charge back into the main hall. Soldiers poured into the room, led by the man in red armor with a winged helmet.

The Onyx Army had come for us.

41

JASIN

Kira ran her hand down the dark stubble on my neck as she gazed at me with a satisfied smile. "We should have done that a long time ago."

"I'm glad we waited. I wanted our first time together to be meaningful."

"It was perfect."

I pressed a kiss to Kira's neck as I held her close. Perfect wasn't enough to describe what we'd just shared. I'd been with plenty of women before, but sex had never been as good with anyone else. Then again, I'd never felt this way about anyone before either.

I loved Kira. I'd known for a while now, maybe since our first kiss, maybe even before that. I could tell she cared for me too, but I wasn't sure she was ready to hear those words yet or speak them back to me. It didn't matter though, because I felt the love between us every time we touched, like an everlasting flame that flickered but would never die. Now that we'd officially bonded, it was even stronger.

At that thought, I remembered the entire reason we were here, which had been easy to forget in the heat of the moment. "While I'd love to keep you here all night and make love to you again and again, the others are waiting."

She sighed and snuggled in closer against me. "You're probably right, but let's wait a few more minutes."

"My pleasure." I ran a hand down her back. "Are you sore at all? Do you need anything?"

"No, I'm fine. I just feel warm all over." She paused and a strange look came over her face. "Do you think I have fire magic now?"

"I don't know. Maybe. Do you feel any different?"

"Not really."

"I didn't either, at first." I paused, remembering the flames that had swept over us. "I wonder if I can turn into a Dragon now. I guess I thought the Fire God would appear to us or something."

"Me too. Maybe he was giving us some privacy." She lifted herself up to a sitting position, drawing my eyes to her full breasts. "Calla said we should go through those doors when we were done."

While the temptation to toss her back on the bed and cover those breasts with kisses was strong, there would be plenty of time for that later. "Let's go."

We reluctantly left the bed and donned our clothing

again, then headed for the double doors at the back of the room. They were thicker than the one we'd entered through, and as we approached they opened with a blast of heat.

The doors led outside near the volcano's crater, which made the night glow orange in front of us. I slowly approached the huge circular pit, where the intense heat was coming from, while Kira hung back. I didn't blame her for being wary, but curiosity drew me forward and kept the fear at bay. Fire couldn't harm me anymore, and the chance to peer inside an active volcano was something I couldn't miss.

I got to the edge of the crater, where a stone ring had formed around it almost like a wall to hold the lava in. The crater went deep into the earth, where dark magma oozed and bubbled and flared up. I could only stare at it in awe, captivated by its beauty and power.

Suddenly a huge blast of lava shot up into the air and I fell back. The heat became so intense I wasn't sure I could bear it. I scrambled back to Kira, who stared up at it in awe. As I followed her gaze, I saw why.

From the crater rose a colossal dragon made of shifting, sliding lava, with bright bursts of fire for eyes. Most of his body remained inside the volcano, but his head and long neck towered over us, while his talons grasped the edge of the crater with an impact that shook the ground under us.

When his massive wings spread out behind him, sending lava flying into the air, I dropped to my knees in awe. The Fire God looked different from when he'd visited me before, but he was even more impressive and terrifying in his true form. Like the other Gods, no one knew his name. It was said the Gods' names were in a language that couldn't be understood by humans, and when I looked upon him now, I believed it. He was alien and incomprehensible and yet familiar at the same time, like this magic inside me recognized that it had once belonged to him.

"You have done well, my children," a huge voice boomed from his molten mouth, which was covered in large, sharp fangs dripping with lava. "But your journey is far from over."

No one would ever call me a humble man, but for the first time in my life I felt it, along with a sense of pride at being called his child. I bowed my head. "What do you wish of us?"

His fiery eyes burned into mine. "You are the new Crimson Dragon, my representative in this world. Serve me well and prove I have chosen wisely."

I swallowed and nodded slowly, feeling the huge weight of responsibility on my shoulders. "What must I do?"

"The others will look to you for leadership and guidance, and you must help them find balance. None of the elements exist alone. Even now, I am surrounded by my brothers. The air above me. The earth below me. The water beside me. Remember that."

That wouldn't be easy, especially when I was the one getting into fights half the time. Not to mention, we still didn't know where Reven had run off to, or if he would ever return. "I will try. But I have to ask, why did you choose me?"

His great wings fluttered, sending sparks flying into the air. "Each of the Gods values different attributes. I look for bravery, passion, and energy."

"There must be dozens of men who represent those qualities much better than I do."

"You misunderstand." His long, reptilian head lowered as his eyes focused on Kira. "We find the mate who will best bring out those qualities in *her*."

Kira's face paled as the God's talons inched toward her. "Did you choose me too?" she asked, though I heard fear in her voice. I was impressed she'd made it this close with her fear of fire, but she was handling it well, all things considered.

"No." His head tilted as he studied her. "Do not be frightened."

She bowed her head, as sweat ran down her temple. "I'm sorry. I've been afraid of fire ever since my parents were killed by the Crimson Dragon."

"In a way they were, and in a way, they were not."

Kira cast me a confused look. "They weren't killed by him?"

"The people who raised you were killed. The people who created you still live."

Kira's hand went to her throat. "They're alive?" she whispered. "Who are they?"

"This journey will lead you to them, but you may not like what you find." He suddenly reared up, his great flaming wings spreading wide. "Only together can you stop the Black Dragon and her mates. Now go. Your companions need you."

Before we could react, the Fire God descended into the lava again and vanished. The sky immediately darkened and the heat returned to a more bearable level. I wiped sweat off my forehead and shakily rose to my feet, then turned toward Kira. She looked like she was about to ask me something, but then a distant scream and a huge rumble drew our attention. The Fire God's words rang in my mind as we burst into a run back toward the temple's doors.

In the front hall, a battle had clearly been fought and lost. Numerous Onyx Army soldiers filled the room, and the dragon statue—which I now realized represented the Fire God and not Sark—had toppled over. Auric and Slade had been captured by soldiers and were on their knees with their hands bound behind them and swords at their throats. Calla lay on the ground bleeding from a gash on her chest, while her four priests hovered over her glaring at the man who pointed his large sword at them. General Voor.

As we entered, every single person in the room turned toward us. "There they are," the General said. "Surrender, and we'll let the priests live."

Rage exploded in me at the sight of Calla's blood, the toppled statue, and my friends being held captive. How dare they come into this sacred place and attack the priests here. These soldiers had once been men I'd fought beside, but now I only saw them as the enemy. The Fire God wanted passion and bravery? I'd give him that.

The heat flared inside me and I embraced it, letting it wash over me until I was burning alive. Blood red scales rippled over my skin as my entire body expanded and shifted and became *more*. My fingers turned to talons. My teeth became fangs. Fire burned in my throat as my long tail flickered. With a great roar, I spread my large wings.

I was a Dragon.

4 2

KIRA

Every soldier in the room fell to their knees except for the General, all of them gasping and crying out. "The Crimson Dragon!" some of them shouted, while others asked, "How?"

Jasin's new form was terrifying and awe-inspiring, and I felt a flicker of fear until he looked at me and his eyes were the same warm brown as when he was a human. And though he looked a lot like Sark, who had haunted my nightmares for so long, he was still Jasin, the man I had given my heart and body to only minutes earlier.

I rested my hand on his side, feeling the smooth, warm scales under my fingers, before turning to the General. "The Fire God has chosen a new Crimson Dragon. Leave now or feel his wrath."

"That's impossible," General Voor said. "Sark is the Crimson Dragon."

"Not for much longer," Jasin growled, with a voice I barely recognized. "Let them go."

The soldiers seemed hesitant, glancing between Jasin and the General, unsure of who to follow. The General pointed his sword at us. "We serve the true Dragons, not these imposters. Kill them. Kill them all!"

Two soldiers charged at Jasin, but he swiped them away with his massive talons. Others raised their swords to Auric and Slade and panic swelled inside my heart. Without thinking I reached out toward them and flames shot from my palms, setting both soldiers on fire. The men screamed, while I stared at my hands in wonder. I'd done it. I'd used fire. And I wasn't scared at all.

Jasin had given me both his magic and his courage.

Slade and Auric jumped to their feet and moved to protect the priests, though their hands were still bound. I prepared to launch more fire at the other soldiers, but then felt a blade bite into my neck and a large presence behind me.

General Voor gripped my arm tight, holding me against his chest with his sword at my throat. Blood dripped down my neck, and he was strong enough that I didn't dare move. Everyone in the room froze, with my three mates staring at me and the General. Auric looked worried, Slade had a stony expression, and Jasin, well it was hard to tell with his new reptilian face, but I knew he was furious from the bond shining bright between us.

"Surrender, or I kill her," the General called out.

"Get your hands off her," a cool voice said behind us.

General Voor cried out as a spurt of blood washed over me. It took me a second to realize it wasn't my own. He let me go and stumbled back, while my heart pounded in my chest as I spun away to face the man I so desperately hoped was my savior.

Reven held one of his swords in his hand and had murder in his icy blue eyes. He stabbed Voor a second time in the chest, then watched him fall to the ground. As soon as the General hit the ground, I rushed toward Reven and threw my arms around him, burying my face in his chest.

"You returned," I said, while my heart nearly burst with relief and happiness.

With his free hand he clutched me tight against him and gazed down at me. "I did."

"Why?"

He shrugged. "I knew you would need my help. Looks like I was right."

"Is that the only reason?" I whispered.

He took my chin in his hand and brushed his lips across mine ever so softly. "There may have been other reasons too."

With their General dead and a large dragon glaring at them, the soldiers all surrendered. Jasin shifted back into human form with a great slithering of scales and a rush of heat. He strode toward me and Reven. "Are you okay?" he asked me.

"I'm fine," I said, touching my neck. It didn't hurt anymore, and I had a feeling the wound was already healing itself.

He gave Reven a sharp look and I expected him to say something rude or angry, but instead he said, "Glad you're back. Don't do anything like that again." Reven only nodded in return.

The three of us rushed over to Auric and Slade, who had already removed the ties around their hands. Auric pulled me close for a kiss, whispering, "I'm so relieved you're safe." I turned to Slade, who wrapped his muscular arms around me in a protective, close embrace. He pressed a soft kiss to the top of my head, before releasing me.

Calla moaned, and I dropped to her side, my panic returning. She was covered in blood, as were the priests who were trying to tend to her wounds with worried looks on their faces. They were her mates, just like my men were mine.

I took Calla's hand in mine. "You're going to be okay."

She coughed and clutched her bloody chest. "No, I won't. But it doesn't matter. I fulfilled my purpose. Twenty years ago the Fire God chose me to be his High Priestess, just like he chose you, Jasin." Her eyes shifted to him, before going back to mine. "He told me I must come to the Fire Temple to prepare for the next Dragons. I've waited for this day for most of my life, and it is an honor to know I could help you both."

Jasin kneeled beside her and took her other hand. "You've served the Fire God well."

Her eyes fluttered shut. "Thank you."

As she faded away, my heart clenched and something burned in me like an ember. Through our touch I felt a kinship with her, like a twin fire flaring bright inside of both of us. I took Jasin's other hand in mine, forming a circle between us, and felt it within him too.

The gift of the Fire God was inside all of us.

While drawing strength from Jasin, I willed it into Calla, praying for the Fire God to help us heal his chosen priestess. Our hands began to glow with the same unearthly orange light from the volcano, as if lava flowed underneath our skin, and the heat became so intense I nearly let go. But I held on, and a second later Calla gasped and opened her eyes. The four priests around us cried out and rushed to her side.

"You healed her," Blane said, while the others praised both me and the Fire God.

"With Jasin's help," I said.

"The Fire God has truly blessed us all," Derel said.

"Thank you," another one said, whose name I had forgotten.

"It seems the Fire God still has more work for you," Jasin said to Calla.

"Thank you both," Calla said, as she sat up with a smile. She cupped my cheek and then did the same to Jasin. "I will cherish your gift and do whatever I can to help you."

"If everyone's good now, we need to get out of here," Reven said, with his lazy drawl. "The Crimson Dragon—the other one—is heading this way."

Fear gripped my throat, but Jasin wrapped an arm around me. "We can fight him," he said. "I can face him as a Dragon now too."

"No, we can't," Auric said. "He's immune to fire, just like you are. We don't stand a chance until more of us can shift too."

"He's right, we need to run," Slade said.

Calla got to her feet, with the help of two of her men. "You must hurry. Go out the back by the crater, then head down that side of the volcano. It leads to the ocean, to a dock where a ship is waiting for you. You can take that to the Air Realm and the next Temple."

She truly had prepared for our arrival, anticipating everything we might need. "Thank you," I said, hugging her quickly. "I hope we meet again."

"We will."

"What about our horses?" Auric asked. "And everything with them?"

"We'll bring them here and take care of them for you," the fourth priest said. "When it's safe, we'll make sure they are brought to you."

"Now go, quickly," Calla said. "There's no time."

43

KIRA

We grabbed our few belongings and rushed through the temple, past the bed where Jasin and I had made love, and out through the doors to the volcano's summit. It still glowed from the lava deep in its pit, but the Fire God was nowhere to be seen this time. We rounded the large crater and battled through the heat that threatened to suffocate us, but I wasn't afraid of it. Not anymore.

That was, until I saw the lava flowing down the side of the mountain. It bubbled and churned and slowly slid toward the base of the volcano, where it met the ocean with a burst of smoke and slowly hardened into new land. *A mix of all the elements*, I thought, remembering what the Fire God had told us.

"This is where Calla told us to go," I said. "But how do we get down?

"I might be able to fly us down," Jasin said. "Although I don't really know how yet."

"That sounds like a good way to get us all killed," Reven said.

Auric's brows furrowed. "There must be a way down."

Slade ran a hand over his beard as he considered. "Maybe I can shift the rock..."

"That's it," Jasin said. "The Fire God said we had to work together if we wanted to succeed. Slade and Reven will form a path for us, Kira and I will keep the fire and heat away, and Auric will protect us from the fumes."

All the men nodded and pride swelled inside me as they made a plan to work together. We moved to the edge of the lava, where Reven sprayed water in a stream, which Slade used to solidify a path of earth. Jasin kept the rest of the flames away and we rushed along the new stretch of land, sweat dripping down all of our faces, and began to descend.

As Slade and Reven continued to create the path going down the mountain, Auric kept a bubble of clean, cool air around us. I did my best to keep the lava and flames back, but I wasn't sure how to use my new powers yet, and I suspected Jasin was doing most of the work.

The dock at the base of the volcano was made of the same obsidian as the Temple and somehow remained completely untouched by the lava, which flowed away from it. By the time we reached it we were all exhausted, sweating profusely, and covered in soot, even despite our best efforts. We stumbled forward toward the boat anchored at the end, its black sails already raised, like it had been waiting for us all this time.

"Anyone know how to sail?" Jasin asked, as we stepped onto the wooden deck of the ship.

"I know a little," Reven said, glancing up at the sails.

Auric looked up at the sails as he wiped sweat off his brow. "I've never been on a boat, but I think Reven and I can use our magic to steer it."

"Then let's get out of here," Slade said, as he cut through the ties holding the boat to the dock and used his magic to lift the anchor out of the water.

Reven shifted the current around us and Auric filled the sails with wind, pointing us north. To the Air Realm.

The boat began moving away from the dock thanks to their magic, and in a few minutes, we were out on the cool water under the endless night sky, leaving the volcano behind. I glanced behind us at the glowing summit and spotted a large dragon flying over it, his blood-red wings flapping once as he descended to the Temple. *Sark.*

This time I was certain he was looking for me. For us.

And soon we'd be ready to face him.

ACKNOWLEDGMENTS

Although I'm probably best known for my contemporary romances, fantasy and science fiction have always been my true loves. I've wanted to write a fantasy romance for years, but was always scared to branch out into the genre.

When 2018 started I decided it was my year of trying new things, being bold, and writing what I love, so I bit the bullet and dove into Stroke The Flame. I absolutely loved writing it and can't wait to see where Kira and her men take me next. But I couldn't have embarked on this new venture without the help of many people, to whom I owe my deepest thanks:

- My beta readers, Lissa Hawley and Amber Swinford. You both gave me such amazing notes and the book improved a thousand-fold thanks to your help!

- Eva Chase, who helped me so much with everything from cover to blurb to plot ideas. I could not have done this without you!
- Lidiya Foxglove and Sarah Piper, my favorite RH cheerleaders - your daily messages keep me going!
- My husband, Gary Briggs, for accepting that sometimes the house is a mess when I'm on deadline but loving and supporting me anyway.
- My amazing readers both new and old - thank you for taking this journey with me! I hope you enjoyed the first chapter of Kira's story!

ABOUT THE AUTHOR

New York Times Bestselling Author Elizabeth Briggs writes unputdownable romance across genres with bold heroines and fearless heroes. She graduated from UCLA with a degree in Sociology and has worked for an international law firm, mentored teens in writing, and volunteered with dog rescue groups. Now she's a full-time geek who lives in Los Angeles with her husband and a pack of fluffy dogs.

Visit Elizabeth's website: www.elizabethbriggs.net

ALSO BY ELIZABETH BRIGGS

CPSIA information can be obtained
at www.ICGtesting.com
Printed in the USA
FSHW010949271221
87201FS